FIVE ACRES AND DEMENTIA

To [illegible]

My best –

[illegible] Mutchler

3/23/84

Chandler Center

The House in 1873

FIVE ACRES & DEMENTIA

How to Restore An Old Texas Farmhouse And Keep Smiling

by AUGUSTA MUTCHLER

Illustrated by BARBARA WHITEHEAD

CORONA PUBLISHING CO. / *San Antonio, Texas*

In memory of my father, Roy Risley

address Corona Publishing Company,
1037 South Alamo, San Antonio Texas 78210.

Library of Congress Catalog Card No. 82-73293
ISBN 0-931722-18-7
Printed and bound in the United States of America

Designed and illustrated by Whitehead & Whitehead

Contents

Like tetanus, the organism that causes construction fever thrives in rural air and, like mumps, it seems to hit you hardest when you catch it in mature years.

John Graves
From a Limestone Ledge

Introduction

THIS BOOK CHRONICLES the experiences of old house restoration by a mature couple high on fresh air and early retirement. For one partner, it was a return to his farm origins. For the other, a city slicker, it was an unmarked trail.

Jim and I started civilized with two fifty-year-old houses in Monte Vista, a historical district in San Antonio, and progressed to uncivilized with the one-hundred-nine-year-old house we now live in. (Trust me: one is enough in this category. Two fifties do not prepare you for a hundred-year-old house. Nothing does.)

City restoration was a piece of cake. The farmhouse has been a career. If you understand country restoration with its unique problems, you can restore a city house and appreciate the fact that you do not also have to prime the pump to get running water.

Jim was brought up on a South Texas farm. He was seven when he had polio; this was during the Depression and money was scarce. He used crutches for three years, and learned to outrun, outfox, and outmaneuver Black Stallion. When he was ten, he got his first brace.

Any man lucky enough to strap on a custom-tailored, twenty-eight inch leg brace every day for the last forty-eight years (remember the choices: paralysis or a pine box), ought to be able to retire to an easy chair, or tinker around his shop making doll houses and tiny cars. Not Jim. Jim has spent his life proving to the world that he can still outrun, outfox, and outmaneuver anyone with two good legs, curly hair, and blue eyes. Today he owns a secondhand Ford tractor.

Public schoolteachers, according to Jim's understanding, lead cushy lives. Short on hours, long on pay, we show up a few hours a day for a few days each week, repeat this for a few months, and get the big vacation. During these halcyon work days, public schoolteachers deal with clean-faced children who are polite, cooperative, and hungry for knowledge. All of this is true, of course. It's the trip back and forth to the psychiatrist that causes teacher burn-out. House restoration is therapy.

The Girls: Lili is a thoroughbred dachshund who claims royal blood. She is known locally as the Baroness. At first glance, Bird appears to be a street mongrel—a cross between a standard dachshund and a Labrador retriever—but was identified by a canine cognoscente as a rare Doxidor Fetcher.

Until three years ago, Jim and I lived comfortably with Bird and Lili in that charming historical district in the big city. We had central heat in the winter, central air conditioning in the summer, and hot and cold running water all year round. We had our choice of utilities—natural gas or electricity—and bi-weekly trash pickup. And in the city, we had connections: sewer connections. The grocery store was a block away, and my school was a ten-minute drive.

Then Jim came down with a terminal case of the bucolic plague, and things were never the same. Two years into his retirement, when he should have been content to listen to the kilowatt hours click away on the meter when he was at home by himself, resting and declining, he decided that he could not spend the rest of his life in the city, and that a little acreage, a big garden, and a few animals would be his Versailles.

I agreed that the house we lived in was too large for one retired person and one public schoolteacher. I reminded him, however, that we had purchased a small cottage three blocks from our house, restored and rented it with the idea that when this day came, we'd sell our big house and move into that charming two-bedroom cottage. When I say charming, I mean that I could vacuum it centrally by standing in the hall and moving the Electrolux to the right or to the left.

Jim said (after having worked on this retirement cottage for six months), "Yes, but the yard is so small." Of *course* the yard was small—another reason to buy it, restore it, and call it home.

He countered that there was no room for a garden, no room for the girls, Lili and Bird,

to run and play, no room for sheep. Sheep? He said that since San Antonio was going through with another and another of its infamous rate hikes, the click of the kilowatt hour gave him heartburn and high blood pressure. On a farm we could save money by the bushel and shoot the finger at inflation (a colorful expression I'd picked up from my students). He said we could raise our own vegetables and heat our farmhouse with wood.

Humor him, I thought. I could drive a few extra miles. But if we looked for acreage, we could also look for a cut limestone farmhouse to restore, which would keep both of us happy. (The bucolic plague is contagious and no respector of age, sex, creed or ethnic group; it zaps one and all.)

After reaching an agreement—a cut limestone house on acreage—we figured we'd just run right out and sign the papers. The first realtor I called said, "Lady, I'd like to have thirty little ol' German farmhouses to sell. I could retire tomorrow." The second and third and twentieth and thirtieth realtor all said basically the same thing, but we started the search anyway for that ideal piece of rural real estate. It made the quest for the Holy Grail look like a weekend armadillo hunt. We figured that somewhere, someone would have one raunchy little old house they wanted to unload.

I found the ad almost immediately. The house was part of an estate and was everything I had ever wanted in a house and less: no bath, no kitchen, no glass in the windows—but potential. My God, did it have potential: faceted limestone, log corncrib rock barn, and it was just the right size for the two of us. It was all there in its pristine dereliction and waiting to be purchased.

It was also sitting on one-hundred-and-fifty prime acres, and the price was slightly less than a half million. I still dream about it.

If we had not run across that jewel of a house early on, we might have believed that no one can buy old houses anymore, and either looked at new ones or thought to build. But there was that house in the back of our minds, out in the middle of all that acreage, untouched by remodelers, and for sale. If one such place existed, then surely there must be others.

In the beginning, we were pretty sophisticated in listing our wants: flexible on acreage, but firm in our stipulation that the house had to be a hundred-year-old limestone, one story, two bedrooms, not remodelled and within twenty-five miles of San Antonio. Some people use booze to reach the same high.

A year passed and we could recite the litany of the ad page. We knew about every old crumbling heap within a fifty-mile radius and all the hundred-year-olds modernized with glitter ceilings and indoor/outdoor carpet. By then, we would look at frame (but not too seriously), two stories, and thirty miles with almost any kind of acreage. When we bought the remodelled two-story, we paid for 3,500 square feet, roughly a thousand of which had to be torn down, and 2,500 square feet of good shag carpet that had to be torn up.

When we first saw this house, I told Jim it could become a magnificent phoenix if someone who cared about old houses would help it out of the ashes. And Jim said, "Sure. And it would hang around your neck for ten years like an albatross before it got off the ground." Later on, he had what appeared to be psychic revelations: every trip by, he'd shiver and say, "I'm afraid we're going to wind up with that house, and it scares the hell out of me."

His psychic revelations proved to be gut-level logic. Who would want 3,500 square feet of house with a monster air conditioner in the attic two of whose ducts traveled through closets to reach the downstairs? (The third duct had been abandoned between floor and ceiling and never finished.)

Who would want a century-old house disguised as a chicken ranch with wall-to-wall shag over termite-damaged floor, and a French chandelier over the tub? And who would want a fantastic cut limestone with a twenty-by-thirty cinder block addition obliterating its face? We didn't, but the devil made us sign the mortgage papers because it was the only game in town.

WHAT WE HAVE LEARNED. . .

1. *People never know how good they've got it* until they swap their fifty-year-old mini-manor for a hundred-year-old ruin.

2. *Be careful what you wish for*; frequently your dreams come true.

3. *Forget the amenities.*

So you used to have a house without holes in the walls. Big deal. Now you've got niches in the wall where an air conditioner once rested, broken windows in the addition that has to be torn down, a plastic-covered cardboard patch in the window of the room you're camping in, a hole in the bathroom floor, and a shaky commode.

Don't bother explaining to strangers who come looking at the ruin that you really used to live nicely with waxed floors and tasteful Orientals. They won't believe you anyway. Your friends will fill in the void by extending sympathy. "My God," they'll say, "how could you take on a job like this?" (Congenital senility.) Or, "I could never live this way." (Me either. We aren't living, we're biding time.) Some will even bring you fresh baked apple pie and spiced tea, and spread a picnic lunch under your trees, and pat your hand and say, "It's all right. This, too, shall pass," and make you feel much better.

4. *Remember that nothing is set in concrete even if it's set in concrete.*

You have a jewel of a limestone fireplace that needs to be firebricked and stabilized. The mason, who is very old, puts the bricks in, and they protrude a quarter-inch past the face of the fireplace.

Your husband wants the fireplace braced. The mason puts a two-inch angle-iron beam across the opening with one side facing the room. You say, "But the angle iron shows," and he says, "You can paint it." That's your clue. Feed the man, pay him off, and hire someone who will remove the bricks, remove the iron brace, and do the job right. You cannot be expected to live in a house with pushy firebricks and a mauve-painted metal bar looking you in the face every time you walk into your living room. You don't get a medal for pain.

Another time you will hang a door, and it will be on the wrong side of the frame. You don't have to rush right to the toolbox and remove the hinges that day. But in a week or two, you'll be able to say, "That door needs to be rehung, properly." Appreciate the fact that, until you get around to it, at least when it's closed it's not in the way.

A friend once remarked, "I don't see how you can do so many things right." Quite simply: we did a lot of things twice.

5. *You can't take it with you.*

If you really want the house, and it appears to be within your price range (or a trifle beyond), there are creative realtors and bankers who will make it possible. If it is totally out of your price range (our dream house for a half million), nothing short of becoming a Hughes heir or a Getty godchild will put your name on the deed.

(The house that was restored in Boston for the Public Television series "This Old House" was backed—financially—by Montgomery Ward; you could call that "money." We were backed by the sale of our city house; you could call that "life savings.")

After you have purchased the house, and there are repairs that might be done by a carpenter or other skilled craftsman better and faster than you are able to work, hire him. If you've got money, remind yourself that you can't take it with you. If you don't have money, remember that your banker can't either. Borrow a little and make monthly payments which will be easier on you than living in the pits for years.

6. *Restoration brings its own rewards.*

Assuming that you have just that state of balminess that is needed to buy an old house in the first place, your joy at finding in the attic a crystal prism, a bone-colored B.V.D. button, or an 1876 newspaper, will far outweigh the intrinsic value of these antique baubles. And your delight in knowing what lies behind a wall, how the bath is plumbed, the walls plastered, and the windows operate, will sustain you through the plastering pits and the wind-tunnel winters.

In the end, if you persevere, you will have a house that rewards aesthetically (eleven-foot ceilings), emotionally (we survived!), and

financially (drastically reduced utility bills). You will have a house that does not look like your neighbor's house, a house that is not made of particle board and pressed paper paneling, and one that was designed and built in harmony with nature. It will allow you to participate in the change of seasons and become more aware of the world around you. Not many new houses offer you these satisfactions.

FIVE ACRES AND DEMENTIA

FOR
SALE

1

First Things First

WHAT TO LOOK FOR BEFORE YOU BUY

ASSUMING YOUR HUSBAND looked at the property one evening when the sky was breathtaking, and a lush pecan crop was at his feet, and he said deeply, huskily, as though it were a barely audible prayer, "I've got to have this place," you may not have time to call a contractor, or your hair stylist, for that matter, for an opinion. Buying real estate is—for most people—an emotional thing that is conducted with the heart and not the head. If you are the emotional buyer, you will probably go into some kind of deep trance once you see the place (and it clicks), and you won't come out of it until the kitchen roof leaks and you find it has for a decade and the joists are rotten and must be replaced.

When you see a house with three remaining walls, the fourth having been carried off by raiding Comanches during the War Between the States, and you say, "Oh, this could be a charming restored house! Nestled under the trees here, new tin roof there, garden over yonder, . . ." stop in the middle and ask yourself where the Comanches live now before you continue your fantasy. You must first repossess the original rocks. Today's rocks are not the same. The mason will say, "Why not face this wall with fieldstone?" which means veneer, which means "not authentic." But if your mental health holds, the place may still be a possibility.

You may make friends with the Indians and they'll give you a rock for Christmas. Obviously, it would take time to work up to this gesture, especially if the rock were part of the foundation of their home. Another, more direct way, would be to offer beads and trinkets. (The natives have a predeliction for Krugerrands strung on 18 kt. gold chain. Nothing fancy, of course: medium weight, and twenty-four inches long should do.)

If, on the other hand, the stones were carried off by some German farmer, forget it. The farmer will say, "Mein Gott, nein. I need dat rock." (He's holding the barn door closed with it; without it, his sheep loose would be.) Go back to your realtor and check his listing, or go with the mason who will veneer the wall; then plant climbing roses or English ivy that will cover the wall in five, ten years. There are simply no brownie points for batting your head against a brick wall, or any other.

If—and I don't know how one goes about this—but *if* you can look at the property with a level head, you might get off with a more realistic idea of cost than the trance victim.

You'll hear the realtor say, "Listen, I'm only showing you this property because I had already made the appointment, but the owner just called, and this acreage will be taken off the market at seventy-nine-five, and—depending on the New York Deal—relisted at ninety even. Since I have already quoted the price, the owners will honor it because we're good friends but tomorrow—well, I don't even know if it will still be for sale. A little earnest money down and we can tie this baby up."

Listen carefully to the pitch. It is true that old properties are not on the market very long, and you can't dawdle around for months. But if, to your novice eyes, it looks like a dog, it probably is a dog and the realtor is trying to turn a fast commission. (The "New York Deal" was not explained.)

Really *good* old properties are often snapped up before they even get on the market. There is such a demand for old houses around our way that the realtor for one property had a list of thirteen family friends who were allowed to bid on the estate. Because we fell down and pounded the earth, she let us submit a bid; we didn't finish first.

Our plumber summed it up: "It's a wonder you got this here place. Mr. Smith must not have known about it." Mr. Smith buys up everything in town with any age to it.

INSPECTIONS AND ESTIMATES

If you are really interested and it looks like something you could handle, a professional realtor will allow you to make arrangements for a walk-through with a contractor or architect.

The contractor will be able to give you a rough estimate for the work you want done and some realistic advice about the work you will do.

It is best to know your real estate dealer very well, and know his qualifications. Some dealers are almost as knowledgeable as contractors and could give you an idea about cost; others are not. If the man says, "With a gallon of white-wash and a couple of tin patches on the roof, this cozy cottage will be ready for a medallion," scratch him and call a contractor. If, however, he says something like, "Twenty-five thousand will keep the rain off your kleidershrank," he may be able to give you a ball park figure, and let you decide if you can play the game.

If time is of the essence, and you can't wait to sign the papers, you can do some fast checking yourself by phone. Get approximate size of rooms, outside walls, etc., from your sales-person, call a contractor and ask for rough figures for big jobs such as "rewiring a seven-room, two-story frame" or "replacing roof joists and putting on a new roof."

If you get the over-the-phone estimates, you can double the figure in order to have a safe margin to work with. If you have a walk-through contractor, and he gives you, *in writing*, his firm price of $27,500 to replace the underpinnings of the roof (lots of termite damage), and put on a standing seam, you should still mentally add thirty to fifty percent to that figure. If you're playing it so close to the wire that you won't be able to afford a $48 vent for the chimney, you will slow down the work considerably and accelerate your temper tantrums.

If you feel up to crawling around in the attic and bellying around in the crawl-space, there are several things to look for. (Good luck in the crawl-spaces, ladies and gentlemen. What not to look for is a pit viper, but you may find one anyhow.)

If the electrical wiring looks like your kids' old tennies, all frayed and tattered, call an electrical contractor for a rewiring estimate.

While you're in the attic, look for little bugs with gossamer wings. Those creatures are called termites and are Trouble #1. Take a knife and jab the roof beams. If the knife breaks, you are looking at petrified pine that will span the attic another century. If stabbing the beam is like stabbing a sponge, you are looking at termite damage or dry rot which is Trouble #2. If the underside of the roof is watermarked, you have (or maybe have had, if it's been repaired) water damage. Trouble #3.

Depending upon the species, your extermination bill could run from $200 to $2,000. Unless you are an entomologist, you probably won't know the difference between subterranean termites and dry-wood termites. Subterranean termites must touch base with soil every day —like Dracula. They are predictable and easy to destroy by just poisoning the ground. Dry-wood termites never have to return to earth for water. They must be gassed, and this is where the fun begins. It may involve two days in a motel for the entire household and two-thirds of your belongings, while the exterminators cut holes in your floors, tape the doors and windows, and board up the porch.

Fortunately, dry-wood termites are fairly scarce. Except that infected lumber was brought into our area some years ago, so you never know. Have the exterminator in *first*, so you won't have holes cut in your newly-laid floors.

In the cellar (or under the house), if the pipes are galvanized iron pipe, check for rust. The plumbing is probably old because galvanized iron pipe has been out of style for some time. If you have propane or butane going to the house in these pipes, ask for an estimate to have them replaced. Assume the pipes are rusty and don't even turn on the gas before the lines have been replaced with new copper tubing.

(Talk to a plumber about propane if you want thrilling stories about houses going up in flames or in one magnificent explosion. "I'll tell you, that was one big fire. Well, the fire department come, but there wasn't nothing they could do but set back and watch. No sir, when it went, it went. Lucky the people wasn't home."

Another entertaining person is your electrician. He'll come down from your attic and say, "Boy, if you ever have a fire, they'll never put it out. That attic has three complete roofs—lots of lumber and tar up there.")

In the cellar check the floor beams with your knife as you did in the attic. Check type of foundation if you can get to it. Few old places will have solid slab foundations as we know them today, but many will have spots of solid base. All milk separator rooms, it seems, were built on granite or on one large mass of poured concrete. Because our kitchen is a combination of smaller rooms (four, including the separator room and a cistern), we have a fourth of the kitchen concrete, a three-by-three corner closed in that covers a deep cistern, and the rest pier and beam.

Foundations in old rock houses are unique. When our bath area was gutted and the flooring removed, Jim saw the suspension system and laughed. The floor joists rested in a rock niche that was created by making the wall wide at the bottom. He laughed and said, "how primitive, how jerry-rigged," until he remembered the floor had been standing for a century and was

still substantial and going strong in every other room in the house. Before one snickers too loudly about old-fashioned construction, dwell on the number of houses being built today that—a hundred years from now—will cause a restorer to marvel at the wonders of particle board, Sheetrock, fake paneling, and vinyl tile.

RESTRICTIONS AND EASEMENTS

In the country, you are relatively free to do you own thing. If you are living on five or ten acres, you're talking "close" neighbors, and you are free up to a point (that point being your neighbor's sensibilities). If you live on a thousand-acre spread, you're talking royalty, and you can do anything you want, short of bucking the Daughters of the Republic. But a five-acre plot is more like serfdom, and you should try to mind your manners.

Building restrictions vary widely. Some rural properties have no restrictions at all. No contractor who worked on our house ever had to get a permit. You could have an open cesspool if you weren't afraid your neighbors would fire-bomb your dwelling some night. One of our neighbors keeps pigs, but he has the pen located so that you don't know he has them unless he tells you. He is a very kind and thoughtful man. However, because there is no restriction that says you can't have pigs, he could have put his pen where it suited him, and if the neighbors got caught in the crosswinds, well, tough beans for them. Some country freedoms are a drawback—to the neighbors.

Rural properties are almost always described in terms of restrictions: "No restrictions—trailers and horses welcome," or, "Acreage in Subdivision" in which case there may be numerous restrictions, some as stringent as in the city. The building materials for the home may be limited to brick or masonry, or the dwelling to be built must not be less than a certain size, etc. This, too, keeps the property value high, and is to your advantage, especially if your acreage is small.

In the city, you have to have a permit to change a light bulb, and in an historical district, not only to change the bulb but remove the light fixture cover. These strict regulations actually bolster property values, but can be vexing to people not used to asking if they may change their trim color or install central air conditioning.

Ask about restrictions before you sign. If you plan to raise horses, check restrictions for that area. You may find, to your surprise, that you'll have to switch to raising gerbils—or look for a different property.

An easement is, according to Webster, "an interest in land owned by another that entitles its holder to a specific limited use or enjoyment." These "enjoyments" can be many things, including the utility company's right to run power lines through your vineyard. Most of the time, however, easements deal with property access: one man's easement is another man's lane.

Easements are not the exclusive property of country real estate, but you are more likely to find them there. In the city, subdivisions have been laid out by someone with a master plan in mind—someone who buys the land and puts in streets that make your property accessible to the Fuller Brush man and the mail person. In the country, you might look at quite a few properties during your search that are accessible only by driving through someone else's farm. An easement is the least desirable way to go home.

If the road to your house is on someone else's property, and the term "road" is loosely used, you might want to find out whose responsibility maintenance will be. If it's *his* responsibility and the road is a battleground of chugholes and pools, you may want to put life jackets in the car to make sure you get home in time for supper during a wet spell.

TAX BREAKS?

The Federal government and organizations dedicated to the preservation of old buildings make a lot of noise about tax breaks. They are making big noises to the restorer of a commercial building and small noises to people who restore in designated historical areas. They are not even rattling a pan to the individual who overhauls a derelict out in the boonies for his own dwelling and aesthetic satisfaction. Our tax man looked at the book, and just kept shaking his head in a negative way. Were we going to open a German restaurant that specialized in sourdough bread? No. Were we trying to borrow money from a historical trust? No. Were we in for some kind of generous tax credit? Leider nichts.

You may write for the tax brochure or contact your local conservation society. If you are eligible for these big tax breaks (i.e., if you are a big investor) you may have your serf or secretary call for you.

CONTRACTS

1. Between you and your spouse.

Agree upon what work is to be done before buying the house. There will be problems enough later on without having to present a petition to the man who shares your checking account concerning the wisdom and merit of tearing down a twenty-year-old cinder block addition that is obliterating the face of a hundred-year-old cut limestone.

Be specific, and be in complete agreement about changes. That cinder block room may not be the only problem. You agree that it must go. The porch *seems* to be no problem. You *talk* about its being rebuilt (after all, without the gingerbread porch, the house is just a rock box). Two years into restoration (and two years into the demise of your life savings), the room is torn off and all of a sudden, Jim thinks in terms of economizing. "Well," he says, "since we won't use the upstairs very much, we really only need a one-story porch." A one-story porch on this two-story house would look like an afterthought, and you suggest several possible disposal areas for that idea. Jim says that we've already spent a mint, and what the hell do we need with a porch over our heads when we'll never use it, and so on.

After several days of heated discussion, compromise. If he can show you a two-story house with a hipped roof and a one-story porch, you might reconsider. You put the girls in the pickup and take a long drive looking for a house similar to yours with one tacky porch. The evening will be lovely. The temperature will be pleasantly warm, and every dog in South Texas will take exception to your truck's being on their road. Lili hisses "Unwashed peasant" at the pack. Bird yells "Yer Mother," and vies with Lili for the window.

You see nothing, between grabbing Lili and rolling the window up to keep Bird from jumping out. After the tour, you will go back to the two-story-porch idea as soon as you can afford it.

Remember to make all decisions early, and work on this area with extreme diligence. You've been married thirty years; you don't want this fun project to stand in the way of another thirty.

2. Between you and your contractor.

The Formal Contract: Be sure the work is spelled out for the big jobs—even the most obvious thing must be in writing or you will be in for big surprises. Your contractor will be finished with the bath and will say to you, "Do you want us to do that back wall?" and you say, "What do you mean, do I want you to do that back wall? Don't we have a contract for you to build a closet in back of the bath?" And he says, "But it's only for three walls," and you know that most closets contain four walls. Silly goose. Not this closet. It contains three new walls (the contracted walls) and one wall that has been standing there for over a hundred years and now has peeling plaster. Don't assume anything is implicit in the contract unless it's written in the contract. You revise the bottom line with an addendum that reads, "Fourth wall—plastered—extra."

At best, you will wind up with a folder full of pink addenda. It is not possible to deal with a contractor without dealing with pink slips. Before you sign anything, think through the work involved; and make sure each step is itemized.

The formal contract will state commencement and completion dates, the sum to be paid the contractor, and the method of payment. It is a good idea to have written into the contract a clause that allows the owner a month in which to live with the finished job before completing the payment (it's only ten percent, but on a big job, that ten percent is large enough to make it worthwhile for the contractor to have a satisfied customer, and it gives the home owner a little leverage).

The Informal Contract: The formal contract will be thirteen typed legal pages; an informal contract will be the work to be done and the price, e.g., "Plumbing pipes to upstairs bath replaced with PVC and copper tubing. $750." Frequently with small jobs this will be enough.

The Verbal Contract: The verbal contract can be as valid as the formal one if you know the contractor. The key is to *know your contractor.* This is not an efficient way to do big jobs, but if the work is simply "replacing the galvanized iron pipe from the propane tank to the house with copper pipe," or "removing the cinder block addition from the face of the earth," it's as good as any.

For all contracted work, listen to your own early-warning system: get at least three bids and

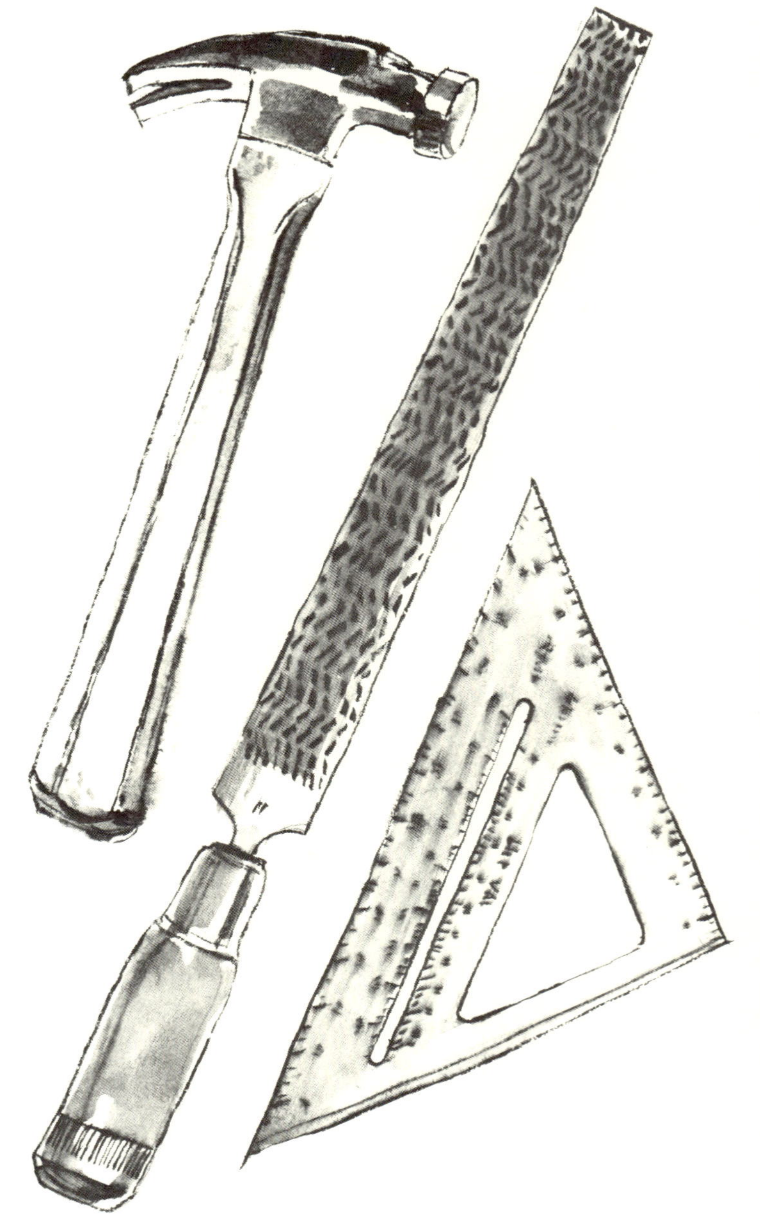

always be leery of a bid considerably lower than the other two. If you have selected three reputable contractors, the bids will be similar; then you will have to fall back on that gut-level feeling you have about each. If you are wary of any one of them, avoid him like the plague. Otherwise, you will turn your down payment over to the contractor one night, and the next night see him on the ten o'clock news spread-eagled against his living room wall with the reporter telling about the biggest drug bust in the city's history. Know, at this point, that you have been had.

If you need extra help in this area, turn to Bird for advice. If she refuses to let go of the contractor's leg, pick someone else.

A NOTE ON MENTAL HEALTH

Remember that restoration and masochism go hand in hand. R. and M. Hand in hand. Take a mental health test or see your shrink and get a grade. The MH score will have to be high enough so that when your disposition continues to decline, the bottom line will just be a crying jag and severe depression—and not a straight-jacket. You can't work well with your hands in a restricted position.

However, if approached with thought and care, I believe that an old house restoration can also strengthen a marriage. Here are just a few of our more poignant marriage strengtheners:

The most wonderfully strengthening and enduring was the "What do you mean you let that stupid-ass plumber put the downstairs lavatory hardware on the upstairs sink?" This took one week to resolve, and we were the stronger for it.

The next best was, "What do you mean we'll put a fifty-year-old door on the downstairs closet, for God's sake. If this place is going to the The Best Little Nursing Home in Texas, it has to be authentic. What do you mean that's what the architect brought? What does he know?" This one was good for two days of lively debate, followed by three days of icy silence.

Another ploy was, "Where in the hell is all the baseboard you took to the stripper? Of course, you took six boards and eight doors. I know that stretches your math. You have only ten fingers. But your toes are untouched. Use them. There are *two boards missing*. MISSING, for God's sake. ONE-HUNDRED-AND-NINE-YEAR-OLD BOARDS—MISSING!" Six hours. How hot can you get over old lumber?

Sometime after the downstairs bath was finished, I would find Jim standing in the dining room just staring off into the bath, trying to figure out a way to arrange his sleeping bag in there.

2
Contracted Work

DECIDE EARLY ON and realistically what your physical, financial, and time limitations are. You may be able to build the finest custom-made window and frame this side of Williamsburg, but if you're a lawyer and you don't have time between court cases, don't string it out for thirty years; hire it done.

Your contractor will not use one, two, or three digit numbers, but speaks four and five digit numbers fluently (and tends to couch his bills in these terms: five thousand, twelve thousand, twenty thousand, etc.).

If the name Rothschild means kin and not candy to you, just call your contractor and say, "Fred Boy, Buffie and I are spending the summer in the Vineyard. We just bought this really primitive Texas farm house for a weekend retreat. Do the job, will you? Understated rococo. Be back in September." If the "job" means carte blanche full restoration, and "Fred Boy" has a graduate degree in engineering from M.I.T., skip the work sections in this book.

If your social circle does not revolve around international airports or Swiss banks, find yourself a local carpenter who will take odd jobs. You'll find yourself writing checks like one hundred and fifty-three dollars, two hundred and nine dollars, or forty-five dollars. This may be such a pleasing pastime that you write two or three checks like this as a warm-up activity before breakfast.

The two ways, then, to have someone else do the work are via a contractor, who will oversee the project from start to finish and who possesses a degree of expertise that you may not have; or with a local carpenter who comes in for a single skill job. He *just* puts up Sheetrock or he *just* plasters your house or he *just* tears off a room. He does not coordinate all the building skills needed, say, to gut the old bath and rebuild from new piers up.

Hire a contractor for jobs too complicated and too technical for rank amateurs to fool

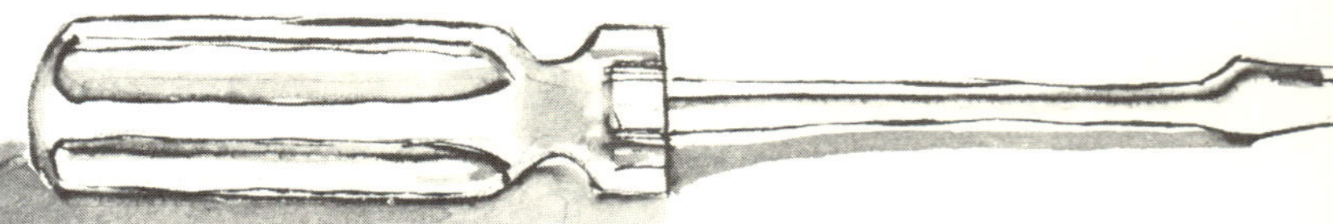

around with. The less difficult jobs can be turned over to a carpenter while you play contractor.

ROOF REPLACEMENT

It is best to stay away from buildings whose roof lines have been changed from hip to gable, unless you have absolutely no hope of finding anything better, and the devil types the contract. If you find yourself in this predicament, find also a contractor whose work schedule is slack, and ask for an estimate. It will be high, but you may decide to go with the flow anyhow.

If you have pictures of the original roof, the architect, in his wisdom, will be able to reconstruct the lines. Without your help, actually. You just keep depositing the money in a Swiss account, the old roof comes down, and a new one goes up; but not without some complications.

If the vice-president of the construction company is introduced as an ARCHITECT, and you are easily intimidated, you are in trouble.

He sends out trim for under the eaves, and you call frantically and say, "My God, Mike. José is nailing up some kind of rickrack. According to the picture, it should be a double ogee at a 45° angle," and he says, "Not to worry. Carefully calculating the diatribe of the hypotenuse, this is the trim on the house and in my drawing. It will look better when it's on."

And you say, "Of course, you are the possessor of Truth," when the truth is that the trim is only half as wide as it should be. You must trust your own eyes (unless you are an uncorrected myopic or have advancing glaucoma) and have the backbone to say, "Damn your diatribal hypotenuse, sir, that is *not* the trim pictured in your drawing or on the daguerreotype." Be prepared to figure proportion.

Measure the drawing of a known (the fascia, in this instance). Then get the scale measurement for the unknown (the under-the-eaves trim) and plug it into this formula:

if 12″ equals 1″ scale,
then,
$\frac{12''}{1} = \frac{X}{3/4''}$ or the scale measurement of the unknown,
cross multiply, or $(12 \times 3/4) = X$
transpose $X = (12 \times 3/4)$
remove parenthesis $X = 8$.

The new trim was four inches wide—it should have been eight inches wide and any layman can pass judgment on that.

Don't be afraid of your architect. Your money is paying for his Mercedes.

You may decide to go with a tin roof because tin looks right, lasts forever, and doesn't encourage fires.

A cedar shake roof would also look lovely and would be authentic, but is a poor choice for country living where the bucket brigade has to ask directions from the sheep in the meadow. Wood shingles act just like kindling, and you don't need another problem in the country, especially if you're trying to keep water in the pipes and warmth inside the house. You won't have time to fight fires outside, much less upstairs.

There are several kinds of tin roofs: the fake standing seam that resembles the real standing seam at passing glance; corrugated tin; and the real thing, a standing seam tin roof that is a thing of beauty and a joy for the next fifty years after it has been waterproofed.

All three tins are used as roofing material for houses, but the corrugated tin brings with it a supply of rain containers. You walk into a house with a corrugated tin roof, and you find, during a wet spell, buckets sitting on top of the dining room table, next to the TV, and slightly to the left of your pillow. Corrugated tin is overlapped, which makes sense, but is then nailed with a lead-headed nail that acts like a gasket/sealer for the nail hole, and keeps water out—for a while. Sooner or later, however, the tin will shift, the nails will loosen, the flood gates will open wide, and you will have one wet house. Let the chickens and sheep and horses keep corrugated tin. They aren't housebroken anyway. The flat tin sheet that looks like standing seam with its little ridges also suffers from the same malady.

A real standing seam tin roof is custom-made, and priced accordingly. The contractor will determine the distance between seams, and have slightly less than a million feet of heavy tin sheets crimped for this job alone. The roof decking will be covered with red rosin paper, a small ridge row nailed down, and the tin sheets with crimped edges butted against it. One long ridge is folded over the other two shorter ones, then the whole mess is folded once again. This takes much pounding, and armies of workers crawling over the roof with maple mallets, but when they have finished, this roof puts a lot of frustration in the life of a raindrop looking for a place to winter.

WINDOWS

If you have strong feelings about birds flying in your upstairs window openings, you'll really have to consider doing something about replacing the hodgepodge of broken windows and aluminum frame ones.

Years ago when the modernization bug hit America, intricately detailed wood frame screens and double hung windows were discarded like kindling. New, modern, maintenance-free aluminum screens and windows (modern man's answer to the servant problem) were installed everywhere, and everywhere they were devoid of character. They were put on country houses and elegant city homes. They were sold to the nuns who run the educational institutions built before the turn of the century and as soon as the ink dried on the fat contract, hundreds of Victorian windows sported slim, shiny frames. However, we are only concerned with the old house that you are restoring.

You know something has to be done, and you have a handful of thermal window brochures —even one that deals with adaptive restoration. The advantages of quality thermal windows are book-length; no painting ever, double pane, tightly sealed, works on smooth-running nylon bearings, can be purchased with optional tinted glass, and venetian blinds between the glass panes (no dusting) . . . the advantages go on and on.

Your contractor will look at the windows and hum a tune as he measures the openings. Eventually he'll say something like, "If we go thermal windows, the openings will have to be closed in 2-3/4 inches on each side. Why not have the old ones reproduced? The cost would be about the same."

Now that, of course, sounds rational, and since the "old ones reproduced" sounds as though it would leave your house looking really authentic, you give it serious consideration with but one reservation.

You hesitate because you don't want real wood windows; your resident handyman is a putty freak. Each year he'll say, "Well, it's about time to redo the windows," and for the rest of the month he'll be removing and replacing putty on the thirty-eight panes. The glass area will be large to begin with, but when the job is finished, he'll have new putty feathered out to within three inches of the middle of the pane. Even well-feathered putty obscures the view.

But you also do not want five and one-half inches of window opening blocked up; you check every other thermal window manufacturer in North America, and sure enough, when they designed their line of windows, your house was not uppermost in their minds.

You have no choice; you must go to reproduced windows. After taking the putty can away from the resident, you think how lovely wood windows will be: gently stained and generously tung-oiled, opening into the room like doors, welcoming summer breezes. . . . The thermal was supposed to do the same but with mixed priorities—the windows opened out, and the screens were inside.

The windows will be beautiful, but because they are not weather stripped they will leak air in the winter. Leak air? More like when the wind blows in the winter the rooms on the north approximate a wind tunnel at testing velocity. You'll have to figure on storm windows, or heavy insulated curtains, or both to eliminate that problem, because you don't want a window edged with copper and felt sticking out into your living space the five or six months the windows will be open. You also don't want dirty socks stuck in the tiny openings between window frame and window, so you have to think of something. (See "Insulated Curtains", page 71.)

ONE-HUNDRED-YEAR-OLD PLASTER

Plastering should be done by a professional. If you are considering doing the work yourself, remember that your objective is to live to see the restoration completed. It's no big thrill to read in the obituary column that you were the restorer of the Last Kraut Stagecoach Stop, who died in the process.

For older restorers, just surviving a plaster job is enough. Especially if you're living in the rubble. The dust infiltrates tooth enamel and does a finish job on the inside of your lungs. If truth were known, Darth and Emily Vader were probably in the middle of an old house restoration when Star Wars began, the plaster dust had already polished her off and left him a respirator case.

One hundred years ago limestone houses were plastered with hair plaster and lime mortar (one-sixth part hair, one part lime paste, and two to two and one-quarter parts rounded-grain sand, in case you want to mix your own). That same material can now be dug out with your finger—the finger with the hangnail.

That plaster has served its time. Today's mason traffics in Portland cement and white sand; in some stone or brick restorations, you must be very careful about the kind of mortar used to repoint outside walls in particular. The more porous, old-fashioned recipes will allow some expansion during cold weather and keep the masonry from cracking and sloughing off. Rely on your architect or stone mason who has been recommended by your minister and three elderly aunts as being reputable. Trust his judgment.

For interiors, Portland cement is used to cover the wall as a base coat, then sifted white sand and crushed marble are used as a finish coat to produce a surface that is as washable and durable as the term "marble" implies. The inside wall will be standing when the limestone has crumbled. Outside, the mortar mix contains more lime to produce a color that blends in with the limestone.

You may have some little difficulty if you have a file folder full of pictures of an old, restored Alsatian house with a wall texture that you want duplicated in your own. Remember that the old plaster was put on by hand and the new plaster will be applied the same way; the human hand hasn't changed that much. There will be a nice roll, even to a smooth plaster finish. Look at the mason's best finish texture first; then go on to something kinkier if it doesn't suit you.

Since this is an expensive undertaking, you could ask to see some of the mason's work. If he hasn't plastered a wall within commuting distance from you, have him do an upstairs room first or a hall or some little cubbyhole so that you can check the texture a day or two after it's finished to be sure it's what you want.

Plaster and mortar colors are deceiving. You may not know what color the grout on the face of your cut limestone fireplace will actually be for four months. Get in writing, signed in blood, that you are paying for matching colors—hold back ten percent of the total bill for a month (have this written into the contract). If the color looks promising at the end of the month, pay the mason. If it looks green or black, but should be buff, call the mason back and have a cup of tea in front of the fireplace while you tactfully mention that that color will never do. Cry.

If he is a sincere mason, he'll get the color right. But do keep in mind that no other material is so devious. It is true that varnished pine will darken with age, but it does this ever so slowly, over a long period of time. Cement, while it is curing, does lots of odd things, and for the longest time can't seem to make up its mind. It may go through a blue period, a green period, and a grey period before finally reaching buff.

When the plaster is right and the mortar colors suit your taste, buy Thompson's Waterproof Seal and brush or spray it all over your house—inside and out. The seal is as liquid as water and winds up on your clothes, on the ladder, and in puddles on the floor, but it is supposed to do what its name implies—make the wall waterproof and keep dirt from becoming part of the picture. It is most important to do the inside bathroom walls (either plaster or exposed rock) and any exposed rock wall no matter where it is in the house. Outside, the seal can be put in a pressurized tank and sprayed on; if planned properly, the spray tank can also be used inside before woodwork and flooring have been finished.

Inside plaster—no matter how reputable the mason—will crack. Don't get all hyper when you see the first hairline crack going from ceiling to floor. With time, your plaster will begin to age beautifully and look as though it belonged to the house originally, which is the look you've been working your fingers to the bone to achieve.

CAUTION: Have the mason replace all the electrical outlet plates. This will only take a few minutes and will save you much toil later on. You'll find that if it's *your* responsibility to put the plates on, by the time you get to it the electrical boxes will have been buried three inches deep in the wall, the cover screws will no longer reach the electrical box, and you'll wind up calling an electrician to bail you out or placing large pot plants at strange intervals around the room.

Also remind the mason that you want all electrical outlets the same height. You don't want to have to look at one box near the floor, and the next one eighteen inches up the wall.

ONE-HUNDRED-YEAR-OLD ROCK WALL VARIATION

After the plaster is taken off the rock walls and you see tons of ivory-beige exposed to the world (and you like rock colors), you may decide to have the wall pointed, and not replastered. This is done frequently by restorers and they almost always take you to that wall first to show you the megalith over the window.

To some restorers, the wall that is stripped, but not replastered, becomes a wailing wall. That wall has worn a plaster coat for a hundred years and has a hard time giving up all the little sand granules.

The biggest problem, however, is the wood trim. There isn't one rock wall in our house —upstairs or down—that is not interrupted by a window or door opening (and there are only two interior walls upstairs that do not contain an opening). This means that you will have facing problems with the wall that was not replastered. The window will jut out a good two inches past the rock, and facings will hang in space. Some very tricky carpentry will have to be done to box in the trim and make a shadow-box type of framing so that the window doesn't look as though it were built by someone who didn't know when to stop.

Also, forget base plugs, unless your electrician can put them in the floor close to the wall or

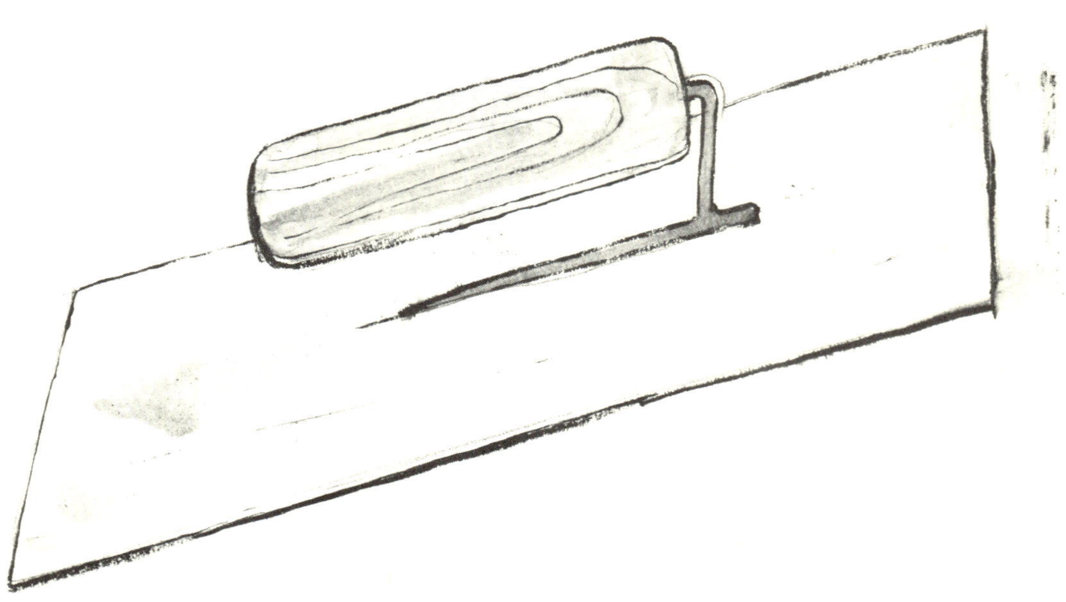

run the wires in exposed conduit down the wall; without plaster, there will be nothing to hide the wires.

NEWER HOUSING: FIFTY YEARS OLD OR LESS

One hundred years ago the mason stayed close to the wall and didn't try to work ceilings; ceilings were covered with car siding or beaded ceiling that did not taunt gravity. Fifty years later, the mason had taken over the ceiling in new construction and nailed metal lathe to everything. Cove ceilings and graceful arches were in.

The hair plaster in a Texas farmhouse is two-inch thick angel food cake. The plaster in a fifty-year-old house will be Portland cement-based; this one-half-inch-thick plaster has the density of granite. The base coat is covered with a thin, hard finish; if chipped, this layer must be covered with spackle. Patching is important because the base plaster will absorb paint unevenly and look rough. The spackle seals the porous base, feathers the edge of the chip, and allows the paint to appear the same all over.

Working with a serious crack or large hole calls for digging out enough plaster around the edge to make sure you are working with sound plaster, and filling in with a special gypsum plaster that contains long fibers. When the patch has dried, cover it with spackle.

The cracks and gouges are the obvious defects in fifty-year-old plaster; the invisible defect is called plaster fatigue, and you won't know about that until you hear things popping even though the popcorn popper is broken and the Fourth of July is months away. Eventually the canopy on the ceiling fan will drop down in the middle of the night and make you feel like Chicken Little. You will say to your husband, "The sky is falling," and only when he turns on the light and sees the canopy resting on the fan motor does he become concerned.

You can check for fatigue by crawling around the attic and running your fingers along the juncture of the downstairs ceiling and the ceiling beam. If you can work your way under the beam with a finger or two, or if you have a flashlight on the other side of the beam and can see light on your side, you're looking at tired plaster. Try to get that fixed before your Orientals move in.

If it's all-out fatigue and you are well-heeled, you call your local mason who will come in, strip the ceiling down to rafters, nail up new metal lathe, and replaster. If it's all-out fatigue and you're *not* well-heeled, you think up ways to keep the ceiling over your head and not on it, without the support of your local mason.

Have your flunky crawl up in the attic and drill small holes next to the ceiling beam. Downstairs, you drill holes through the plaster that will hit the beam square in the middle; put in a large washer that catches the tired metal lathe and a large screw that will hold a little weight;

refill the ceiling, plaster, and paint. Repeat a thousand times if it is a big area.

Another method is to drill holes on either side of the beam and thread heavy wire through the holes, digging out plaster so that the wire pulls the mesh tight to the beam; fasten the ends of the wire around the beam in the attic. Repeat five hundred times. This leaves rabbit ears up there but no one but the squirrel who lives in the attic will be able to see them.

CAUTION: After the lathe is secure, and you are patching the ceiling plaster so that it no longer looks like the cratered surface of Mars, be very neat with the gypsum plaster. That material is a mason's practical joke on the unwary. It looks like a powdered material, you pour it into a container like a powdered material, but once it meets water, it becomes rock and there is no reversing that transformation. Be sure you scrape off any bumps and mountains unless you want the ceiling to look like an upside-down Swiss Alps. IT WILL NOT SAND OFF.

PLUMBING

If, during your fix-up campaign, you are removing floors or moving walls, be sure to take a long hard look at any exposed plumbing. In fact, it would be a good idea to invite a dependable plumber out to look at what you've bought anyway. (By dependable, I mean someone who has been recommended to you as a good plumber; that does not have anything to do with his standing you up twice before he makes it out for this third appointment.) Budget into your restoration as much replacement plumbing as you can afford. It will be cheaper to have it done while the rest of the work is going on than it will be two years later when the pipes burst and take with them your hall ceiling and floor.

Get familiar with PVC, the plastic pipe that has revolutionized the plumbing industry. The handyman who was interested in replacing his own water pipe before PVC was invented, had to know the measurements to within a fraction of an inch, have the equipment to thread pipe (or have it threaded), and know how to fasten joints together (if you screwed a pipe into one fitting, chances were good that you were also unscrewing it from another).

Since PVC came along, anyone can lay pipe, estimate the distance with the naked eye, turn corners, bend it to use up slack, or glue in another piece to add length. The only tools needed are a hacksaw, a bottle of chemical cleaner and one of solvent.

PVC is polyvinyl chloride, but probably the clerk at Handy Dan will hesitate a minute before sending you to the plumbing department if you ask for that. Everybody refers to the new plumbing pipe as PVC. There is even a line of outdoor furniture made from this material. (Actually the chairs and chaise lounges look like the scrap bag from a big contractor's last job, but never mind, people buy it.)

Short of some builder or street maintenance

crew ripping up water pipes that service a subdivision of twenty thousand souls, city water is a pretty dependable commodity. If the pipes are good inside your house, chances are that when you turn on a faucet you've got water if you pay your bills regularly.

In the country, water is free. It's the equipment that gets it out of the ground and into your house that socks it to your budget.

In the city you just run a tub full of bubble bath and luxuriate. In the country, you run a tub full for Bird's bath and all of a sudden as she is wallowing in Johnson's No Tear Baby Shampoo, the water will sputter, then turn rust, brown, and mud, and will flow no longer. The three-thousand-gallon cistern will be dry, and Bird will be rinsing off in the dregs. The submergible well pump is dead, and you will have to borrow water from your neighbor to keep going until the well can be pulled and the pump replaced.

(Borrowing in the country isn't quite like your city borrowing either. You don't take a little measuring cup to your neighbor and say, "Listen, I was right in the middle of a batch of pizzelles. Could you lend me a cup of sugar?"

In the country, you knock on your neighbor's door and say, "Pardon me, but Bird was taking a bath and we seem to have run out of water. Could we borrow five hundred gallons until tomorrow?" at which point the neighbor joins his four hundred feet of hose to your three hundred feet and runs the hose to your cistern, thus keeping you from moving into a motel or going broke on bottled water.)

Even if you have a new well pump and a tight cistern, you must make sure that all water pipes are protected from the cold. It doesn't matter if it's 104° in the shade, if you've moved to the country, and you depend on well water—your well water—to keep you in coffee, go to your local plumbing company and throw yourself on the owner's mercy. Say, "I am a city slicker who just turned. Sell me your best foam insulation for exposed water pipe." Buy as many feet as you have exposed pipe and a few extra, plus a roll of sticky silver tape two inches wide. Split the tube of insulation, slip it around the pipe and wrap it with tape.

A neat little trick used by instrument mechanics and electricians in tight places is the little tape ball—get your flunky to make these for you. When you are lying on your back in the July sun working on PVC or standing on an eight-foot ladder wrapping electrical wire, you're not going to have time, or be in a jolly mood, to make your own. Pull off twelve to eighteen inches of tape and roll it back on itself until you have a tiny little ball that can be slipped freely around

the pipe. This is just as handy when you're working with electrical tape. The only difference is that you need smaller pieces, just four to six inches long.

SEWER SYSTEMS

Country sewer systems are called septic tanks and, when new, are less trouble than old lines in the city. With old tanks, be wary of moss-covered sand in back of the garage during a five-month drouth. Eventually the damp place will become a murmuring brook which will signal the demise of the septic tank. The plumber will bring the Honey Wagon, pump the smallish tank out, and replace it with a large round tank too beautiful to be buried beneath the clothesline.

Septic tanks, like everything else on the farm, have to be fed. They are fed yeast that grows and multiplies. Each time you dump a bucket of ammonia or Clorox or Lime-Sol down the drain, you kill off a few billion and have to put a few more into the tank. You can imagine that yeast friends do not come cheap.

City restorers have sewer hookup which is not as trouble-free as the public water system, but it's not a septic system, either. In old districts, besides antiquated pipes, you will have big trees with marvelous root systems to contend with. Find the grease trap outside and know how to pry open the cover. Eventually the drain will become clogged and a power-driven Roto-Rooter will have to be used to cut roots that feed in the sewer pipe. This is not uplifting activity; only if you're severely strapped for cash do I recommend doing it yourself. Actually it takes two people—one sitting on the ground next to the grease trap feeding the wire into the pipe, and another pressing the foot feed and unwrapping the coiled wire from the ground worker's neck when it goes haywire with its little backlashes (about every 49 seconds). It is better to pass the buck (or fifty of them) and have this done for you.

PLUMBING FIXTURES

If you are interested in buying old bathroom fixtures, haunt antique shops and junkyards. Almost every town has a street somewhere lined with them.

You will find your four-footed bathtub in one such place; the showroom will be a fenced-in enclosure covered with vines and will have spare tubs leaning against the post out front. You might find a tub half filled with dirt, with only one small chip in the corner. It will be even cheaper than a new tub.

Buying an old tub isn't the trick. Buying the hardware for an old tub is the trick. In your average big city, there are two thousand salesmen selling plumbing fixtures and hardware who will get a blank look in their eyes and shrug their shoulders when you say, "Fixtures for an old claw-footed tub, please." No sooner do you get the words out of your mouth than the salesman will just mosey off to another customer and act as though you are waiting for the men to take you away in a white jacket. Forget buying in person unless you live in Massachusetts—or live in Texas but own a Lear jet. Order *Renovator's Supply Catalog* (see Apendix). You simply cannot start a home without this book.

The big ornate lavatories are more likely to be lurking around in some antique dealer's garage. Get to know the dealers on a first-name basis. Each time you pass by a store, pop in and say, "Well, my dear, have you found that smashing Victorian sink yet?" and she'll rattle her brains plenty, especially if you have a loud voice and her shop is crowded. Act disappointed in her; act as though she *promised* to have it on display today. Leave your phone number. She may want to get you out of her hair.

PROPANE GAS

If you've just moved from the city to the country, you have probably never met propane gas. Almost everybody in the country uses it, unless the whole operation has gone electric—which may be the reason the previous owner sold out and went on relief.

You can't fuel a light bulb with propane, but you can heat water with it and use it to fire your bathroom heaters. Electricity for heating is extravagant. It is also subject to power outages. If you just stick to electricity for light, ceiling fans, and cooking; wood heat for the house; and propane for water and bathroom heaters, you will be in pretty good shape if the power is shut off for a while. In the winter, you could cook up a pot of something on the wood stove, but in the summer, you won't feel like much more than cheese and crackers.

Propane has unusual little properties like settling in corners or between walls, which make your most macho plumber nervous. There are regulations now that say you must cut a rectangular hole below the wall heater and cover it with a louvered vent so the propane won't stay in its little corner and sulk but will have more breathing room. This could mean the difference between your being able to detect a leak and your not being able to detect a leak and your whole restoration going poof.

Have a plumber check all gas pipes. Better still, have a plumber replace all galvanized iron pipes with copper tubing and give the whole system a clean bill of health. You'll sleep better nights.

The last accoutrement to propane heat is a propane tank. Butane tanks—not much used any more—are buried in the ground. Propane tanks are always left sitting around in your back yard. It looks tacky, but it's the law. In a week or two you'll get very tired of looking at it, and after a month it will hurt your eyes. Plant shrubs around it, or build a fence or curvy rock wall that hides it, but do think of something.

ELECTRICAL

Be as concerned with electrical wiring as you are with propane gas and wood stoves. If the wires in your old house crumble in your fingers, have the house rewired before the threads give way and electricity starts osmosing from the light fixtures.

Never take for granted that an electrical wire is a dead electrical wire unless it is carrying a lily and you can see both of its ends.

There is a little gadget with two wires and a small light that will help you determine which wire is viable. Don't use your wet finger to ground the wires or you'll be carrying the lily.

When you are tearing out closets and other things, don't get the tin snips and start cutting away. Always show respect around electricity.

If you don't understand electricity, call the electrician. If you do understand electricity, call an electrician. If you are an electrician, you will already have the breakers pulled and the crumbly wires replaced with Rolex.

Have a checklist drawn up before the electrician arrives. When you get the bill in the mail, it will be too late to ask him to replace a plug.

1. Closets.

If he puts a new (or old) fixture in the closet, where is the switch going?

2. Ceiling fans.

Ceiling fans must be cross-braced. This is done from the attic side in a one-story dwelling or in a second-story bedroom, but between the ceiling and floor for downstairs rooms, in a two-story house. When you have the floor torn out and the wires are being replaced, have the cross-bracing nailed in for every room even

if you don't plan on ceiling fans. Later on you might want one, and it will be too much trouble to tear things up again. Once is enough. Just cut a 2 x 4 to fit between the floor/ceiling joists and nail through joist—close to the electrical box.

3. Light fixtures.

Decide on the kind of lights you want. Recessed fixtures are expected to leak heat and cooled air, but with wood heat and no air conditioner, this is not as critical as it might be with central air. Have the electrician check all old fixtures for crumbly wire. Unless the electrician buys the light fixtures for you, be sure you have everything there and ready for him—otherwise you will be looking at a return performance at twenty-five dollars an hour.

4. Attic.

For years, our attics have been almost as much a part of our living space as the living room or kitchen. (There were times out here when the attic was preferable to any living space we might have on the first floor.) We have folding stairs that go up to the attic. Accessible attics are wonderful places for storing junk you can't bear to part with, or to live with. They may also house important things like your insulation, air conditioning ducts (if you have central air), and your attic ventilating fan, and on occasion be a playing field for your exterminator.

So have your electrician put a light in the attic while he's installing the attic fans. Have him put the on-off switch for the attic fan at a convenient height to be reached on your feet. If you have to throw a rope over a rafter and shinny up to the top to disengage your fan, you're not playing with a full deck.

TELEPHONE INSTALLATION

It is best to bring Ma Bell into the act early. Even if this means paying for an extra trip, it is cheaper than a big disappointment after you have waxed the floor and polished the telephone bench.

Decide which room or rooms will have to have phones (our phones are singular—one phone in the hall because we waited too long).

Tell the telephone man what work is to be done, and what is to be torn up and replaced. Have *him* figure out when you are to call him back (when the floor is removed? after the bath has been gutted?).

When the time comes and he rolls back in with his truck, say to his face at least three times, "This is an historical house. When it was built, Ma Bell was just a little cylinder. I don't want any more wires on the outside than I can safely stomach looking at on a daily basis." Three times. Emphasize "historical house."

After he tells you he can staple the wire (to the cut limestone) up the side of the house and run it through the bedroom window, throw a fit. Stamp your feet. Let your eyes roll back in your head, clutch your heart and yell, "No, no, no wires on my house, do you understand?"

If you haven't frightened him too badly,

he'll regroup his thoughts and say, "Well, ma'm, we can bring the wire onto the property on those poles in the next field, run them to the vapor light, and bury them from the pole to the cellar."

Release his throat, straighten his collar, and say, "Thank you."

After he catches his breath, he will say, "But we don't bury them." You bury the wire. It will be cheaper in the long run than burying the hatchet between the telephone installer's shoulder blades.

Ask how deep to bury the wire. He'll say that Ma Bell's specifications are two feet, but since you are doing the work, six inches will be enough. Before you finish, six inches will be more than enough. He also says he'll leave a little extra wire. After much time spent with the shovel, you consider cairns piled over the wire, but discard that idea before the sheep trip over the rocks and threaten to break the line.

You decide on subcutaneous. However, the "little extra" he leaves will be long enough to put mainland China on your party line—ask that he not be so generous because the extra wire has a mind of its own and wills itself free of small ditches. Your final ditch looks like the river Nile to accommodate the surplus.

. . . AND A NOTE ON CONTRACTOR'S TRASH

If you have had thirty squares of wood shingles taken off your roof—shingles that were covered with three more layers of composition —make sure the contractor plans to remove them from your driveway. You could take them to the field and burn them—a BIG job, but possible, if the neighbors who live downwind of you aren't home. Also, debris left lying around for any length of time becomes irresistible to mice and snakes. Have the phrase "broom clean" written into your contract. We did, and each evening the trash was picked up, put in a trailer until it filled up, and then taken to the city dump. Before leaving each day, one workman would waltz around with a broom for a few minutes. Nothing fancy, but it kept things clean enough so that we didn't have rats in our pie safe.

3
Restorer's Work:

OR, THE MASOCHIST'S HANDBOOK

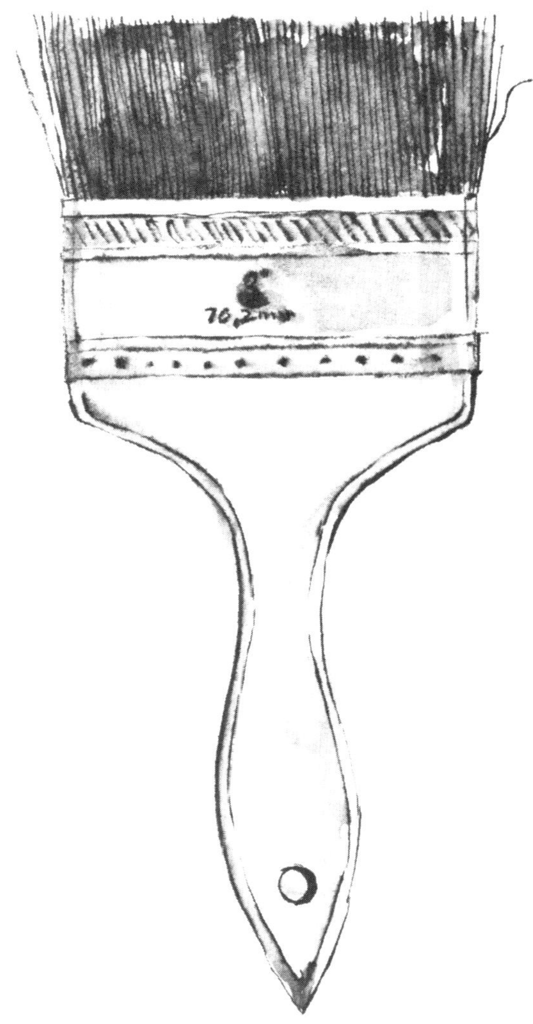

RESTORER'S WORK

A RESTORER WHO doesn't value long fingernails and manicured cuticles can do a lot—and safely—to defray the cost of restoration.

You will save big bucks doing the possible—tearing out and cleaning up, stripping woodwork, painting and doing floors. Although some of these things seem to be small potatoes, they wouldn't be if you had a union man standing on your ladder.

Don't attempt the tearing out without a specific "OK" from your architect or knowledgeable contractor. You may be attacking a load-bearing wall that will get even with you by cratering on your head. Most contractors are more than willing to advise the do-it-yourselfer. You tell them what you feel up to doing, and they'll tell you the easiest way to go about it (assuming you have asked them how to go about it). Or they'll tell you that it's not possible, and you'd better shelve that idea.

FLOORING

Most old Texas farmhouses have five-inch-wide pine flooring. If it is still good, the pine will be as solid as hardwood. If it has been fodder for termites, you'll have to replace it with new longleaf pine.

Take a small piece of the old flooring to your local lumber yard/mill and ask that it be duplicated. The new flooring will be about one-sixteenth of an inch thinner than the original which will call for a heroic sanding job if you start replacing in the middle of the room.

Pick sunny days with low humidity to lay pine flooring. Eat a hearty breakfast. Dry boards can be drawn up snug with a wedge. Boards full of moisture are devious; they'll look good until the humidity drops, then they'll shrink and the gaps between the boards will be wide enough to float a boat in. Do the best you can with the pine flooring, picking the right kind of weather, and nail one board snug against the next. You can leave the job with a good conscience, but you will still have gaps. A month later, you'll notice that two boards aren't speaking to each other. That is the nature of a pine floor that you must learn to live with.

Don't get a can of Weldwood out and say, "Well, that will never do. I'll fill these cracks in myself and have a smooth floor." Don't bother with Weldwood. It's work to fill in the cracks, then re-sand the filled area, then re-stain the sanded area, then vacuum the long, dried pieces of Weldwood out of the floor as soon as the weather has gone through the damp-dry cycle a few times. The floor is better off, and has the appearance of old flooring if it is not too well done. Leave the gaps between the boards, and stain the entire operation with a mixture of Duraseal stains: one part Golden Brown (221), one part Spice Brown (237), and four parts Natural (200). This will give a light but mellow look to the face of the board and leave a darker color in the gaps (it will take a long time to brush the Duraseal in the crevices, but this is important; otherwise, you'll see raw wood and that's not pretty).

Use this Duraseal formula on a piece of scrap wood first; if it doesn't blend with your old woodwork, use a teaspoon as one unit, and vary the proportions of the Duraseal stains. Cohasset Colonials stain is also a fantastic product that can be used on anything—including the floor—and comes very close to duplicating the patina of old wood. This stain must be ordered; they are, however, prompt with delivery.

If your floor was damaged and mistreated long before you bought, you may have spongy old floors, with plywood on top of that, then asphalt tile on top of that, then foam pad and wall-to-wall shag carpeting on top of *that*. If so, strip it all down to the plywood. The original floor (what's left of it) and the plywood will act as subflooring to your newly-milled pine. Put the pine down and you have two additional layers of protection between you and the cold air under the house.

The only problem with this system arises when your flooring comes in contact with original door facings that have not been removed. Facings, by rights, should be put in after the flooring, to seal off raw edges and give a finished look. When you lay your floor over existing floor, the facings will be overpowered by the raw edges of pine boards; this is the one area that must be meticulously filled. (But not with Weldwood. I am not anti-Weldwood; Weldwood does have its place, but that place is in the shop, not on the floor). Use the natural paste wood filler that does not dry as quickly as Weldwood and does not become brittle and pull out over a period of time. Fill the gaps next to the door facing and wipe off the excess. A week or two later, refill and sand. Two or three applications should bring the filler up to floor level, ready to be stained along with the floor. This takes care of an all-new pine floor.

Replacing just a few boards, instead of the entire floor, causes different problems. If you replace some of the boards and keep a good portion of the old floor, the thinness of the new flooring will cause little dips in the floor, but that can be taken care of with a good floor sander (see note below). The old floor will have gaps that will break your ankles.

This is where the filling comes in. You can use rope, but if it's a big job, you'll need enough to supply a rodeo; or Oakum (*Old House Journal* mentions it, but no one in Texas seems to know what it is); or paste wood filler. Sherwin-Williams is one of the few companies that still sells paste wood filler by the gallon. A few weeks before doing your floors, call your local dealer and reserve a couple of gallons. They may not have it in stock, and it will have to be ordered. You don't want to have to sit around and wait a week before you can finish caulking your floor. (Woodcraft also sells paste wood filler, but by the quart.)

Use the filler straight out of the can to fill in the big areas. OK, mix the filler a little; stab it a thousand times with a screwdriver. Then dig out a big glob and put it on the can lid. Take a putty knife, and work the filler until it becomes plastic; then cram it between the boards with your index finger and relief thumb. After you have finished the gaps, mix the remaining filler with the rest of the liquid in the can (it should be of a consistency to brush on, so you may have to add a little turpentine or paint thinner), and brush this liquid filler on rough areas, nail holes, and gouges; then rub off with burlap. This is drudgery, but stay with it; the next step is re-sanding, and when the filler is dry and solid, it's even greater drudgery to sand off.

The mixed flooring will present other finishing difficulties; you will have one-hundred-year-old wood, then fifty-year-old wood that was put in when the house was wired for electricity, then new wood. Staining these three will raise you to sainthood. It might be better to go with Glidden's Floor and Deck Enamel. There is a blue/gray called Flint Blue that duplicates the color of the old lead-based favorite, or you could go white.

If the plaster and ceilings are white, white floors will produce a room that demands sunglasses. After a year and a half of plaster grit sanding the area between your toes, an all-white room is a natural high. Even without furniture, you can sit in a clean corner and meditate upon the mysteries of "restoration," or, "What drove me to it?"

NOTE. Floor sanding: If the sanding has to be an all-out effort, such as smoothing the unevenness of a combination old/new floor, rent a floor sander and hire a local carpenter to operate the machine. A big floor sander is not for the fly-by-night do-it-yourselfer. You will plug it in, flip the switch, and find yourself pinned to the wall by a three-ton machine that is digging a hole in your floor. Only by astute movement of your only free foot are you able to kick the plug out of the wall and save yourself. Just get someone else to do the sanding—you can fill in and paint the floor yourself.

After sanding, filling, and re-sanding, give the floor one coat of paint and let dry well enough so that when you walk on it, you won't leave Yeti tracks in your wake. A day or two between coats should leave the floor firm enough so that you can apply the next coat. The idea behind the application of three coats in rapid succession is that the paint layers chemically bond and create a more durable finish than three distinct layers that might have a tendency to flake. After the final coat, let the floor sit idle for a week or more before moving in furniture.

The all-new pine flooring is a different story, and again this is for the restorer who would like to save money doing it himself. Buy two grades of aluminum oxide sandpaper, medium (120), and fine (220) grit in the 9 x 11 sheets. At the same time, buy a yard of fine grit flooring sandpaper (100 2/0) that is too wide but can be trimmed to fit your Rockwell sander.

Use the black flooring sandpaper on your biggest problems—an unruly ridge you'd trip over if you didn't get it down, or a splinter that needs to be nipped in the bud. Then re-sand the area carefully with aluminum oxide medium grit or this area will take stain unevenly. After eliminating the worst blemishes with the flooring sandpaper, sand the entire floor with medium grit, then fine grit aluminum oxide.

Sanding 50,000 square inches of raw flooring with a 4 x 4 hand-held orbital sander will make you realize that perseverance helps in your restoration, but not as much as Catholicism. Catholicism, however, helps only if you were brought up in a church with wooden kneeling rails. If your parish cushioned the blow of genuflection about twenty years ago with foam rubber, you're not much better off than a

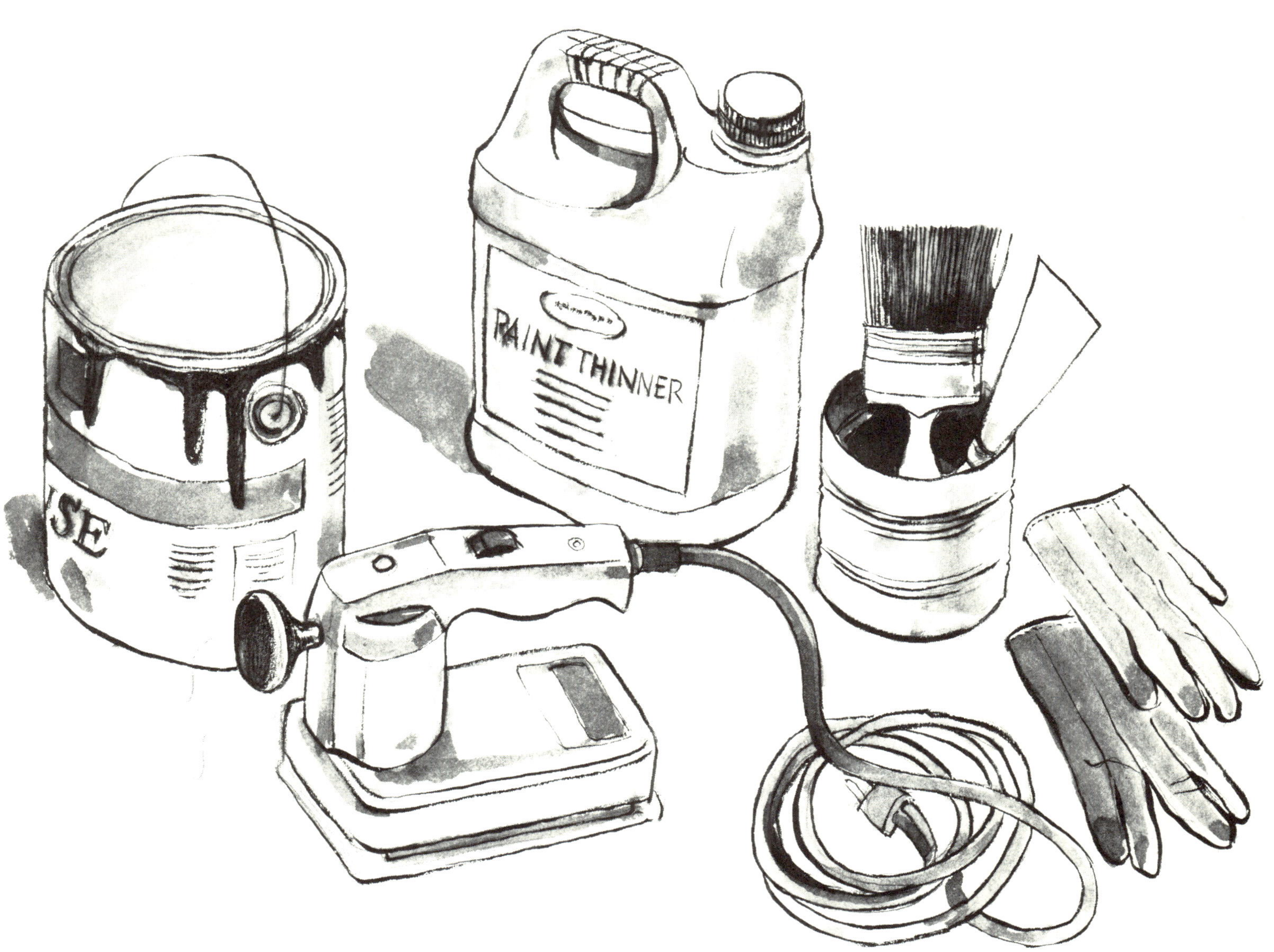
PAINT THINNER

Methodist or Christian Scientist. Foam pads on kneeling rails produce soft Catholics by taking all the agony out of kneeling. But if you have known smooth oak that dimpled your knee caps, you are way ahead of the game and are ready to sand two to three hundred square feet of pine at one kneeling.

Just remember that the big machine, improperly manned, will eat these new floors up. Unless you want to pay a professional to operate the sander for you, the do-it-yourselfer is well advised to stick with the little stuff and suffer through.

ONE SMALL PRECAUTION: Durasealed floors watermark. If you put a glass down overnight, you'll have a white ring on the floor in the morning. If you put a pot plant down, you'll have a black ring in a week. If you Duraseal and then apply two or three coats of thin polyurethane varnish to the floor, you won't have this problem. You'll have other problems: scratches. Repairing a scratch in varnish is much more difficult than repairing white spots on sealed wood, but the floors look nice. I have never lived with polyurethaned wood floors, but a friend who does have them says they dust mop like a glass floor. She is very pleased with them. (She also does not have small children, big dogs, or ubiquitous cats; she probably doesn't even have dust bunnies. But she does have pretty floors.)

If you are apt to drag a chest across the floor with a nail in its bottom that digs a trench in your hall floor, don't even check the price of Glidden's polyurethane varnish. It is useful, though, if you want to do a dining room table or sideboard you know will suffer from Kool-Aid damage the first time your kids have company.

When redoing a newer house—one that is fiftyish, say—you may find a kitchen or breakfast room with chipped original linoleum that is in bad shape. Stripping the linoleum is no problem, but removing the felt and mastic underneath is a challenge.

The first time I was faced with this problem (linoleum glued to an oak floor), I tried mineral spirits, alcohol, paint stripper, and, finally, the belt sander with coarse grit sandpaper. In three hours, I had cleaned less than twelve square inches.

My uncle dropped by and asked if I had tried water to remove the mastic. I like my uncle. I did not laugh out loud. I brought a little pan of water to the breakfast room, halfheartedly splashed it around, and stopped to have a cup of coffee with Henry. When I returned to the job, the mastic and felt came up by the box full.

Slip a putty knife or a wide-bladed spatula under the mess and you can clean a floor as fast as you can scrape it up and carry it off. Water *is* the answer.

With the second house, I used a mop and

bucket and slopped water everywhere until it puddled, had a coffee break, and cleaned a breakfast room and kitchen floor in less than two days.

WOODWORK

If you buy an old house and decide to strip woodwork, take two aspirins and call your physician in the morning. If the pain persists and you insist, remember: you were warned.

Only crazy people strip woodwork. I know that's what you see in all the slick magazines—mellow old wood stripped of its lead-based paint by leprechauns; but unless you've got a rich supply of little people, you've got a big bunch of trouble ahead.

You'll get halfway through (with some folks it might not take this long), and say, "My God, this is punishment. It will take two years to finish the job." It will be too late then; a house half stripped and half painted is for the birds, and you won't be able to bring yourself to paint the stuff you've already stripped.

The only safe way to strip lead-based paint is to use a chemical solvent or use a heat gun that gets hot enough to soften the paint but not hot enough to vaporize the lead; otherwise you will breathe the fumes and die. You can also sand the paint, breathe the airborne particles, your teeth will fall out, and you will die.

The best, most efficient way to strip paint is to remove the trim and doors, engrave a number on each piece and fastidiously record numbers and original location in a leather-bound book, the whereabouts of which is known to you, your lawyer, and at least three witnesses. Stack the things in the long bed of a Toyota pickup and take them to a commercial stripper who has a vat full of bubbling chemicals and somebody else's sluffed-off lead paint. This system does not turn gum tissue blue. Lead poisoning will.

The only drawback is that not all wood-to-be-stripped can be removed from the house without simply tearing it down and starting from scratch—old scratch. The window openings remain intact as will the nineteen-inch-thick door openings, and because the vat-stripped wood will come back so clean, it will make the job of in-place stripping all the more difficult.

However, if you decide to strip woodwork and you borrow a pocketknife from your flunky to remove a big hunk of paint from a window-sill and accidentally run the tip under a ledge and put a little notch in the blade, and the owner of the knife pouts—tell him everybody and his dog would have seen that apple green paint in the corner of the window, but hardly anyone at all will see his knife blade.

If he has a free-floating anger and fixates on the notch, refer to the Woodcraft catalog or Brookstone. (Dont ask me why only Yankees publish tool catalogs—maybe peddling to the South is the only way they can keep navy beans on the table.) Order—even before you look for paint stripper on sale—a complete set of shavehooks. If you really want to be professional, buy two sets, or at least an extra of the one that has three straight sides, and another extra of the one that has one straight and one curved side. These are the most helpful, the most frequently used, and the most frequently found at the bottom of the box dull and crusted with paint. Send them to your helper with the whetstone who sharpens them for you, because a dull shavehook is frustrating.

In one catalog the copywriter suggests dulling the edge of the shavehook before stripping paint. One can only hope this copywriter is in therapy and gets help before he does real damage to himself. Lead-based paint on woodwork cries out for a sharp shavehook.

If I were stripping a mahogany Queen Anne table covered with varnish, I could understand dull shavehooks—or no shavehooks at all. If the finish is varnish, no paint, the thin cheap paint stripper will do just fine. After the chemical solvent soaks in a few minutes, sprinkle sawdust over the surface, wait another few minutes, then wipe off the resultant goop with a rag or rough steel wool. Repeat the process until your varnish is gone.

Either dull or sharp, shavehooks are dangerous tools. Keep all of them in a cardboard box or a basket so that you do not step on them, or, when you're crawling around the floor, kneel on one. No point asking for trouble.

Shavehooks for any Surface

PAINT STRIPPER

Even if you buy the heat gun that softens but doesn't vaporize lead paint, you will still need paint stripper.

All paint to be stripped is located on the vertical or horizontally overhead. There is no such thing as a flat, convenient surface to strip. Of course, the windows have the bottom horizontal board, but that paint has already been dissolved by the sun over the century. The horizontal overhead board is still covered with fresh, tight lead.

Only the thick, orange paint stripper can be painted on with the expectation that it will stay where you put it. The really liquid (and cheaper) stuff will run down your arm and eat your elbows if allowed to stay on long enough.

Paint stripper, like most all paint products, will be on sale from time to time. Read the ads in the paper, and wait until the price goes down before buying your supplies. Paint stripper in its natural habitat sells for slightly more than aged bourbon. Sometimes the paint stripper will be reduced to half price; buy ten gallons for starters.

After you have stripped as much paint as possible from the woodwork, the last step is sanding with medium grit aluminum oxide. The most important part of your equipment at this point is not the sander but the face mask that keeps paint vapors or dust from your lungs—the kind of face mask that is approved by the National Institute of Occupational Safety and Mining Enforcement and Safety Administration. The face mask/respirator comes with cartridges and prefilters.

When you finish sanding, vacuum the floors thoroughly, wash your clothes separately, and clean the face mask of dust. The dust from lead-based paint will settle on floors; the dogs will walk on the floor and lick their feet, and you will have sick pets. If lead poisoning is detected soon enough, it can be treated, but treatment is painful. Don't subject yourself or your pets to this hazard. Keep them away from the area you are sanding, and take the necessary precautions to keep the dust out of your system.

If lead-poisoning is evident, and if your pet survives, the lead will not leave the system without treatment. Don't sit around with a sick pet and say, "Old Rover made it this far—he'll probably get over it." He won't. Take him to the vet, and yourself to the clinic for blood tests.

Besides paint stripper and sanders and respirators and brooms, you'll need:

rags
coarse steel wool
medium to fine sandpaper
sharp needles
a bottle of alcohol
a bottle of Mercurochrome
a box of Band Aids
current tetanus shot.

Avoid handshaking during this period. Just let people think you are ill-mannered, rather than have them squeeze living, medium-grit sandpaper.

PAINT

Your contractor will guide you in your choice of trim paint, but maybe not well enough. He strongly recommends Olympic Stain because it is a good serviceable outside stain, affordable, and available almost everywhere. Only after you have chosen a color, and it has been applied by a hired painter to the roof trim two stories up (see note below), the contractor mentions his bias that Olympic is number two. Cabot's Stain is number one and more expensive. If you are redoing a house with the idea that you want to treat it as nicely as possible, look into Cabot's Stain. However, in all fairness to Olympic, we have used it on all wood trim outside, and inside on the wood walls in the dining room, kitchen, and one bath. We are very pleased with it. Stain laced with linseed oil does not blister, which is a real advantage in a warm climate. An added advantage is the fact that Olympic Solid Stain contains enough pigment to cover new wood and old paint equally well.

If stains and enamels could be compared to fabric, the stains would be velvets and the enamels would be satins. Either stain—Cabot's or Olympic—waterproofs porous wood while allowing it to breathe. Enamels, on the other hand, produce a hard, shiny surface that will resist heavy traffic. Generally, people do not go around pawing window trim or overhangs, but the door will be pushed open a million times by grubby hands.

For your outside doors, take a board covered with the stain you have chosen for your house trim to your Glidden paint supplier, and have him mix up a quart of his best outside enamel to match. Two good coats of enamel are the least you can do for your doors. You could give the doors one coat before hanging, and the second coat—very carefully—after it fits the opening.

(NOTE: Second-story trim work is for the professional painter who trained with the Wallendas, has never known dizziness, and walks the scaffolding like an Iroquois. If God, in His wisdom, had intended for older restorers to paint the second-story trim, He would have put sloe gin in our Geritol and suction bunionettes on our feet. Two stories up is *definitely* somebody else's job.)

PAINT, INSIDE TRIM

Because the interior wood trim—after it is stripped—is exquisite, there will be little left to do. However, you will need some kind of common color in order to blend in new wood with the old. The vat-stripped wood will be very dry and will absorb more stain than in-place-stripped wood causing the former to come out darker.

You can use an Olympic Solid Stain (Chocolate) paint bucket with a cup of dregs left over from doing the outside trim. To this, add an inch or two of turpentine and swirl the whole business gently with a swizzle stick. Wait a minute while the pigment drops back to the bottom of the bucket; then just tip the edge of your brush with the turpentine mixture.

This very light stain is all that the old wood needs for color. Be a little more insistent with the mixing when you do new wood or when you are working with old wood you didn't do an A-1 job of stripping. The Olympic pigment will hide what you don't want your worst enemy to see and makes the whole thing—well-stripped old wood, not-so-well-stripped old wood, and new wood—compatible.

You are working toward a satisfactory match with your stain, when, in the real world, there is no such thing. Old wood looks ravishing; new wood looks new. It's enough if the colors are in the same ball park, say, brown and light tan or beige. Worry if it comes out brown and purple or beige and black.

Several days or a week after the stain dries (or a month later if you're strapped for time), paint on a coat of interior tung oil. If you're doing a whole house, buy the oil by the gallon. Don't just slop it on everywhere, but do get enough on so that the wood at least looks wet. Leave overnight and wipe off any remaining tung oil early the next day—don't wait longer because it will dry on the surface of the wood. If you wipe it off much sooner than that, the old wood in particular will not have enough time to soak it up.

Tung oil is the answer to the amateur's wood finishing problems. Tung oil feeds the wood and allows it to breathe. (I'm with you, Clyde; I've never seen even a hungry naked board take a deep breath, but this is what the experts will tell you; it's important that wood be preserved but allowed to catch a breath of fresh air.)

Tung oil may be brushed on (if you have a lot of woodwork to cover that is the only way to go), or you may rub it on with a cloth. The nicest thing about this product is that it will not be intimidated by dust or foreign matter unless it is applied too liberally and allowed to dry, in which case it will hold as much dust and as many insects as rosin. Another advantage is that you will not have drips and runs on your finished project. If the dull, untreated look does not please you, you may apply as many coats of tung oil as you have energy for—the more coats, the shinier the surface.

CAUTION: Tung oil is poison; do not use it to finish children's toys or to dress a salad. Woodcraft sells a special finish for salad bowls and breadboards—you could use this on toys as well.

OLD DOORS

The wood in most one-hundred-year-old doors is so beautiful some photographers of old houses just stand around taking pictures of them even before they do the house. Before the photographer arrives, but after a door has

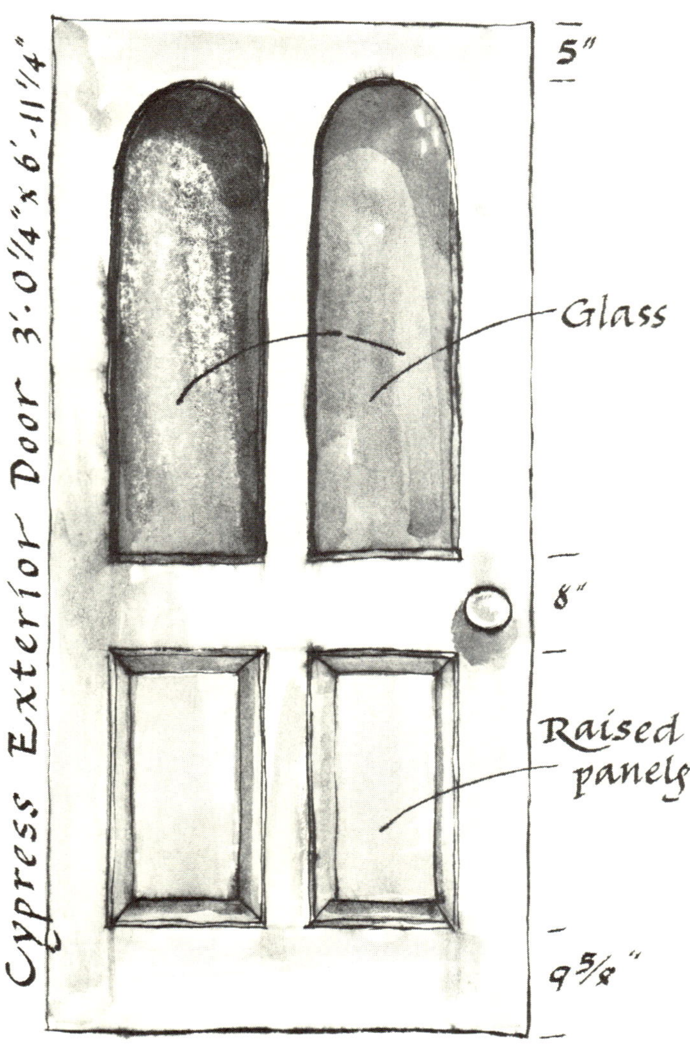

been vat stripped, it needs to be reworked. The glue is usually tired and the hardware needs to be cleaned.

You rework an old door very carefully. Hammer out all dowels holding it together, lightly sand all edges, and reglue. Fill the dowel holes with glue and replace the old dowels with new. Screw holes for hinges may have to be drilled oversize and dowels put in under the hinges. Replace the trim that was floated away in the 1919 storm and feed the door two coats of exterior tung oil before refinishing it.

If you have a lot of doors to rework, it is very helpful to have an extra door—so badly damaged that you can cut it up and not feel guilty about destroying something of value. Use the wood to patch the doors that were cut off to accommodate shag carpet. If that two-inch piece is replaced with old wood, the patch is much less obvious than if the patch were new white pine.

If you have a front door with missing glass panes, you will have to see about glass replacement unless you want to use the chicken mesh that covered the openings when the door was nailed to the back of the garage. Make poster board patterns for the glass to be cut, and present them to the owner of the only glass shop in town. Ask for heavy glass for an antique door. She will look bored and tell you it's against the law to sell window glass for a door; the law allows tempered glass, safety glass, and Plexiglas for this purpose. She stocks Plexiglas, which sounds gross, but before you leave, at least look at it.

Also ask about beveled glass. You haven't lived until you've seen sun hit a bevel and explode the color spectrum all over your floor. This is one happenstance money can buy, and one of the few things that, scattered on your floor, doesn't have to be vacuumed or mopped.

Ask for an estimate for your four small pieces of glass with a two-inch bevel. The owner will say that beveled glass is no longer sold, and you counter with "Then what's put in all those fancy doors going in new houses?" and she'll hedge and say, "Well, the work has to be sent out and it's very expensive."

Stiffen your backbone, make eye-to-eye contact, and say, "Madam, you are dealing with a salaried public schoolteacher. Give me a ball park figure." She'll look at you with greater respect, of course, but with a voice edged in futility will say, "OK. A week ago a man brought a mirror in to be beveled on two sides and the charge for labor alone was $125." Thank her and ask when your quarter-inch-thick Plexiglas will be ready.

We bought Plexiglas for our back door. It was a practical solution to a large expanse of open space. That door gets jostled by cordwood coming in and the ash hopper going out. Plexiglas beats replacing flimsy glass panes every time wood hauling gets out of hand. But there are drawbacks. Plexiglas scratches easily. Unless you are very careful with your paint brush when you paint the door (or extremely agile with a razor blade if you're *not* careful with your paint brush) you will wind up with razor scratches where the paint was. Eventually your well-painted door will end up with scratched and dull-looking panes. If you have a few cobwebs inside to match, and you plan to rent the dwelling as a spook house on Halloween, the Plexiglas may fit into your scheme of things very well.

We chose laminated glass for the front doors. Laminated glass presents no safety problems once it is installed. The problem with laminated glass arises before it is installed—arises, actually, at the shop. Laminated glass is just that: two sheets of real glass with a Plexiglas core. When the glass is manufactured, someone at the mill stamps a little trademark on the core that will be forever bonded between two panes of glass. There is no razor that will cut deep enough to remove it; no ammonia strong enough to expunge it. Some glass shops do shoddy enough work to include that writing on your piece of glass. For your front door. If you let this slip by, visitors will read trademarks on your glass panes while waiting for you to open the door.

When you take your glass patterns to the store, state specifically that you do not want any writing on your glass. Repeat it for the lady who takes your order. Have it written—large—on your work order. Let them know that you prefer paperback mysteries to laminated squiggles. (Even if you *liked* reading glass panes, how involved could you get with the plot?)

Otherwise, laminated glass seems to have the best features of Plexiglas and real glass. It is safe. You can razor off as much paint or exterior tung oil as you need to, and have clear glass to look through. Plexiglas, although safe and less expensive, doesn't come within a country mile of that.

LUMBER GRAFFITI

There will be many times during your restoration that your resident handyman will be working with new wood—either replacing flooring that the termites have pigged out on for the last hundred years, or reworking a staircase that has suffered modernizing from the fifties on. In either case, your resident carpenter will have to use the tape measure to get concrete figures.

When he starts measuring floor boards, he isn't likely to work with more than one at a time, and he will call a new number to you, the flunky, as you cut the board on the sawhorses under the shade tree and push it through the window. No problem here.

The problem arises when he does the stairs. He jots down a half dozen measurements with a stub pencil on scrap lumber and carries it to his shop. Then, when he cuts and works the step risers, he will systematically write on the front of the board:

so that when it's nailed to the stairs, it looks like the first page of a cryptographic journal.

Discourage this activity. If he's into writing and record-keeping, buy him a notebook, or a clay tablet, or string with beads, but tell him to keep the marks off the front of the board. He can go to literary lengths on the back of the board, giving a little history of the house, the condition of the stairs, how the weather was affecting his arthritis, and the exact minute said board was nailed tight—but not on the front, because *you* will eventually have to sand it off.

FENCES

If you and your neighbor decide to put up one section of fence, buy leather work gloves and an extra can of Band Aids. If you're into masochism, buy a posthole digger. If you're not fond of pain, and you're having any kind of fencing put up on your property, ask the contractor how much he'll charge to dig the holes with his tractor and auger. If it's fifty cents a posthole, you shouldn't even hesitate.

If your neighbor is an experienced fence man, he'll know how to line up posts by sighting, stomp them into the ground with a six-foot iron bar, and stretch and staple wire. When stapling, be careful not to hammer the staple too hard or it will cut the wire.

Up to this point, you have worked hard, but there was no really dangerous work (barring cardiac arrest). Stretching barbed wire is dangerous work. If, when the wire is being stretched, it breaks, it will whip and coil and strike anyone standing in its path. It has the potential of a flying machete. Stand far back (in another field maybe) when the barbed wire is being pulled, and approach the fence to staple the wire down only when you know things are secure.

ONE SMALL CONTRIBUTION TO CONTRACTED FENCE BUILDING: OR, BE CAREFUL HOW YOU ANSWER WHEN YOUR FENCE MAN ASKS A QUESTION.

We had two hundred feet of six-foot-high, chain link fence across the front of the property that had the warmth of a federal prison farm. We contracted to have it torn down and a cedar post fence built in its place. Larry, the contractor, asked if we wanted to strip the bark off the posts or if his men should. Jim volunteered.

The big corner posts were four times as big as the line posts, and, as I went into the second hour on the same side of my first post, I wondered out loud why Larry didn't use smooth creosote corner posts as he had done on the other fence in back. Jim said, "Because I told him everything needed to be cedar—I thought that's what you wanted."

When I said it would have been OK to have used smooth creosote posts, he said, "Well, that wouldn't have looked worth a damn—I told him we wanted it to look rustic." Jim was heavy into rustic.

The finished fence was beautiful, but just remember: If you are ever given a choice—to strip the bark off cedar posts or have the bark stripped off cedar posts—choose the latter. A professional cedar peeler knows more than you do.

4

A Bucolic Interlude

IF YOU ARE RESTORING a house in the country, before your restoration is tightened up you will know what it is to live with nature.

Everytime you bathe, you can figure on sharing with a grasshopper, and one of you will drown. Everytime you open a cabinet, it will bring back memories of *Charlotte's Web*. And everytime you approach the trash pile, you will know in your heart of hearts that there is a snake at dead center.

CATS

Cats are necessary farm equipment. You cannot be expected to live the rural life without them; do not let the head honcho dissuade you from your belief. It is true that cats eat mice and birds. I personally do not have anything against either, as long as they stay in the barn and the trees respectively. As long as the mice do not pig out on Grape Nuts and make funny signs in the whole wheat flour, I don't care if they eat a little sheep food in the barn. But cats will be cats and Jim and I do not hassle them if they wish to supplement their Purina Cat Chow with Mickey's cousin five times removed. And my advice to birds is to fly faster. Otherwise, you have a lot of messy feathers lying around.

Cats are essential to a tranquil rural environment, to keep the dreaded snake population at zero growth. Snakes enjoy the out-of-doors as much as you do and frequently sun bathe next to the barn, take a breath of air under a board in the field or next to a log by the water tank.

All country snakes are dangerous, country lore to the contrary notwithstanding. All country snakes are descended from a loose pit viper and a python and are referred to in the vernacular as Vippies, who will either strike you dead or squeeze you to death.

Not only are they fatally ugly, snakes do not make good pets. You can't walk out your back door and say, "Well, good morning, Virgil. Did you sleep well last night coiled up there

in the hot water heater closet?" when Virgil is either trying to strike your ankle with his forked tongue, or squeeze the breath out of your body.

And those little green guys who stretch out on the potted Norfolk Island pine wearing sunglasses and exposing their little white bellies—don't be fooled by their playful attitude. They are as dangerous as the bigger ones. When you're running for cover, the clothes line or a string of barbed wire could be in your way and do as much damage as Virgil.

Buying a book on snakes doesn't help identify them either. The snake books are all beautifully illustrated and the descriptions correct to the last scale. However, when you—out in the field, so to speak—sight one, you're not going to be interested in things like, "This one is covered with an intriguing diamond pattern from rattler to just short of his tiny ears, with the interior part of the diamond being slightly richer in hue than the outlining." What you *are* going to be interested in is the message from brain to lower extremities which says, "Feet, don't fail me now."

Country lore doesn't help. Snake books do not help. Cats help. In return, you must take care of them—have them neutered and given shots. Without the shots, they could die of some dread disease. Without the spay, you could die of bankruptcy. Cats populate at a rate 2.3956 times greater than guppies. You don't need thousands to keep your farm free of snakes. One litter will do.

Those with pizazz can be named something smashing—but for all the loyalty a cat shows, you can skip the familiarity, and call them Katze Eins, Katze Zwei, Katze Drei, or Uno, Dos, Tres, and so on, if you let things get out of hand.

Try to encourage them to headquarter in the barn and just work the area around your house. If they get on the road and are smashed flat as a pancake by the passing pickup parade, they won't do you much good. Then, instead of shots for the ungrateful felines, you could have bought a bottle of aged Scotch to counteract the snake bite once you've been bitten. A dead snaker on the road is no threat to the snake population, and when Shifty sees this turn of events, you can bet *he* will try to go home again —to your home.

INSECTS

Just when you have company some winter evening, and there is a chill in the room, and you close the insulated curtain, a small spider will drop down on your shoulder and curse you for destroying his home.

Country houses are fair game for every manner of insect known to Darwin, most of whom feel free to do a rotating residency in your curtains, the crevices in the couch and along the perimeter molding at the ceiling. Mix a quart of Spectricide (1/2 ounce Spectricide to one quart water) and put in a hand-held spray. Spray the tops of your curtains, and the crevices of your couch. Buy a telescoping duster, spray the wool dust head, and wipe the ceiling trim without bringing in the big ladder and making a day's work out of it. The trim doesn't need to be saturated. Just give the spiders a whiff of the Spectricide every couple of months. Spectricide discourages the nesting instinct.

If insecticides bother you, buy a telescoping duster anyway and frequently run it around the perimeter of the ceiling. A tumble bug is to a spider what escargot is to a Frenchman—yummy—and if you allow cobwebs to live on your ceilings, they will soon contain dozens of tumble bug shells and a few fly bodies. You will have a hard time explaining these things to the decorator from Dubuque who comes to check Texas interiors.

FLEAS

If you are anti-insecticide, buy bear grease or whale oil or something equally repugnant to fleas because they are no respecter of residential preference; you can have fleas in the city and you can have fleas in the country. No matter where you live, they are difficult to get rid of. If you let them get so far as to colonize your rugs, hang it up and call an exterminator.

I am not particularly fond of pesticides. I would rather talk quietly with the colony's leader and suggest an alternate life style. A bale of alfalfa would make as good a foundation for his empire as anything the house has to offer, without interference from crepe-soled shoes. I have tried. I have offered to help them move, but when I address the leader, I find ten or fifteen of his followers eating my ankle. "Let us reason together" is not part of the flea's experiential background.

Because Bird has allergies right up to her eyes, her allergist recommended frequent baths, no sweets, no chicken skin, and no fleas. Everytime she goes outside, I say, "You do not have permission to have fleas, Bird," and she always nods that she understands, but brings them back anyway. She has cat friends outside whose fleas are not my responsibility. The only way I can imagine keeping up with flea control on four semi-crazy cats is to put flippers and fins on them and let them tread water in the rain barrel all summer. (Of course, this would cut down on their effectiveness in keeping down the snake population.)

The flea spray that is used on both girls is supposed to kill fleas. What the spray does in the real world is to give the flea population lustrous hair, cavity-free teeth, and hyperactivity. In no way does it endanger the fleas' civil rights. Well, if you can get a direct hit with the spray, you may drown one or two, but, all in all, it does little damage.

If, at some early point in your restoration, you line a closet with genuine aromatic cedar boards, save the scraps. If you can plane some cedar curls, you can stuff them in a pillow case and make a comfortable bed for the girls that does not attract fleas. The girls aren't too wild about it either, but if they are tired enough, they'll put up with anything. If you can't make curls, gather up all the little chips and sawdust and put them in small bags, and tie one or two to their bed. (If things get bad enough, you might hang a few on your own.) These little cedar chips thrown in a bag, do not a bed make. Little cedar chips in a pillow case are as comfortable as a gravel drive, and you wouldn't like that either.

FLEA CONTROL IN SUMMARY:

1. Put up signs in four languages: English, Spanish, German, and Arabic. Letter the message carefully: "Fleas, go to your own home." You may assume that at this point, they know your home is not yet their home.
2. If they ignore the warning, bring out the big gun. Spray everything in the house with Spectricide except the dogs' water dish. Wash that bowl and refill. Place on a clean towel along with the food bowl. You don't want the girls to ingest insecticide with Purina. Remember your quarry: fleas, not dachshunds.
3. Spray the girls frequently with the veterinarian-approved spray just to keep the flea spray people in business and help support the economy.
4. Get a big club, and keep a sharp eye.

COUNTRY CLOWNS

You may never have an opportunity to play around with a bumpkin skunk (pray that you never have an opportunity to play around with a bumpkin skunk), but they are charming and entertaining to watch at a great distance.

Our skunk, Preppy, comes home early in the morning looking like a charming and gay, high-spirited Irishman headed for his favorite pub. He waddles to the tractor shed and holes up under an enormous stack of old lumber. (This looks pretty cute now, but if we ever want to use the old flooring and joists to make furniture, it may not be so cute when people enter the living room, admire the rustic coffee table, and ask where the odd smell is coming from.)

It's OK to enjoy these little fellows at arm's length; the big trick is to discourage them from approaching your living space. A skunk living under your house may react to sudden noises or other disturbances in a way that will permeate your dish towels and closets. You can double the trouble if you have to keep your dogs away from them. Assuming there is always that possibility that Preppy will get Bird before Bird gets Preppy, we keep four large cans of tomato juice at the ready.

(Nota bene: You do not snap your fingers and say, "Oh, Fig. Bird just got perfumed by that damned skunk," go to the kitchen and make yourself a Bloody Mary. The tomato juice is for the dog—not to drink, but to bathe in. Maybe after the tomato juice bath, and she still smells funny, she'll need the Bloody Mary.)

DEER

In someone else's field, deer have a spiritual quality—standing in that pastoral setting in the early morning mist, silhouetted against a muted green field. They quicken your heartbeat, and give you a glimpse of Elysium while driving to work.

In your field, deer have the quality of eating your lettuce in the morning, nibbling your beans at noon, and munching down on your corn at dusk. A six-foot high, deer-proof fence is the only safeguard for your vegetables.

THIMBLEWEED, OR SHEEPHERDER'S BANE

One summer day, we got our lawn mower back from the repair shop in San Antonio. Jim was like a kid with an early Christmas. We had taken the mower in a month earlier, and our thimbleweeds had needed cutting then.

Thimbleweed is also known as Mexican hat, *gallitos*, cone flower, and black-eyed Susan. Sheep do not like thimbleweeds, and neither do sheepherders. Thimbleweeds grow so thick and strong it is almost impossible to get through a stand of them when they are full grown; practically impossible to cut them with the mower because the stalks will stop the International Harvester in its tracks; and totally impossible to pull them up by the roots because the roots have already established credit at Peking Feed and Seed.

An alternative is to poison them, which kills the plant but doesn't do away with the stand of dried stalks strong enough to fish with; poisoning is also not practical with the lambs in residence.

Our solution was to hire Bud, our neighbor, to shred them with his tractor (before Jim's tractor arrived), then cut them frequently before they got too big for the International Harvester, which was what Farmer Jim had been doing, and why he so desperately needed his mower returned.

A week went by and the shop said the mower was extremely ill and needed something like a short block which they did not have, but for a price, a BIG price, could order.

Jim called the next week to see if the part had arrived, but it hadn't, and he gave them a short course in Parts Follow-Up.

He called the third week to check on the mower, gave them a refresher course in Parts Follow-Up, and reminded them that he had twenty (emphasized the twenty as though it were fifty) years experience in supply.

He called the fourth week to check on the mower, gave his refresher course, reminded them of his twenty years, and said in exasperation, "Son, I'm up to my ass in weeds."

Son, on the other end of the line, tired of Pompous telling him how to run his business, said, "And I, sir, am up to mine in lawnmowers." We got the mower back—a week later—and the bill was almost as much as the mower cost originally.

BULL NETTLE

Bull nettle is difficult to get on paper, but if you have to deal with it at all, it is much better in the abstract than in the field.

Bull Nettle (*Cnidoscolus texanus*) is a deceiving plant, one that looks much like the kind of greenery you pay good money for at the violet farm, place in a window with plenty of light, water and fertilize religiously, and watch die. Bull nettle grows with a total disregard for regular rains, sufficient food, or relief from the summer sun. It sits there—low to the ground—with soft green leaves decorated by tiny white dots, charming white blossoms, and poison secreted somewhere on its lascivious little self.

When we first moved to the country, I was trying to tell my Uncle Henry about the nettles we had in the field; he asked if we had bull nettles. I told him, of course, we had a field full of plants that were sticky and uncomfortable when I had to round up the sheep, but he seemed skeptical, and again tried to explain the concept, "bull nettle." Finally, in exasperation, he said, "If you've got bull nettles, you'll know it." The plant I was trying to describe was the Texas Prickly Poppy. Henry was right; you'll know on first contact if you have bull nettles. You will believe a coral snake is chewing your tibia, and when you see there are no snakes in sight, you will remember what Henry said.

Bull nettles will cause skin to sting for several days, and leave red welts. Become familiar with a drawing of a bull nettle before picking wild flowers.

SHEEP: A CITY SLICKER'S FARM IDYLL

In the city, Jim and I had both been tired of smelling exhaust fumes in our living room and tired of hearing the EMS unit pick up the bodies at our corner (we lived on a very dangerous, busy street). Besides these aggravations, Jim resented the fact that he spent time, effort, and money growing carpet grass he couldn't eat, and trimming edges for someone else to enjoy. His little backyard tomato crop took less effort and produced vegetables that made a chef salad worthy of the name.

His grand idea was to buy sheep and let them take care of the grass and weeds, while he took care of his garden.

Five months after moving to the country, Jim bought ten sheep—five ewes and their five little ones. They came from a beautiful Hill Country farm long on acres but short on grass, to Jim's retirement farm that was short on acres, but long on weeds. They thought they had died and gone to heaven.

The ewes were scrawny and all the lambs seemed to have only one ear. Some people call it "notching," but nobody ever notches down to an animal's skull. I called it "cutting off an ear," and believe the fellow who did it either ate a lot of lambs' ear stew, or had a Van Gogh complex.

Actually, one ewe did have two ears, and one had a true notch, just a small piece missing from the ear, but the rest were totally unbalanced. Charles Lamb was the most outgoing member of the flock, and the only baby boy. He grew horns in retaliation.

The lambs were shy and skitterish at first, but it wasn't long before they caught on to their new environment and especially to their evening ritual; so much so, that often they would be lined up outside their shed, singing a chorus or two of "Baa, Baa, Maa." Sometimes when I went out to feed them, they'd still be grazing, then one white face would look up, then two, then ten, and lambs farthest out in the field would leap over thistle and thimbleweeds to join the chorus line to the shed. In two weeks time, they knew the routine, so I thought it perfectly safe to put out medicated food designed to keep stomach worms at bay, knowing they would eat with gusto and without question.

Except that one night. That night I went out the back door only to be greeted by dusk. The lambs were picking their teeth in the field, and just nodded a friendly acknowledgement as I passed by on the way to the feed trough. I figured they'd hit the trail as soon as the food hit the pan, but there was no distant thunder to announce the lambs' arrival at the shed after the four pounds of stomach worm pellets were distributed evenly in the three troughs.

I stepped outside to call them, and happened to see the two fifty-pound feed bags that I bought earlier in the day, broken open, and at least fifteen pounds of feed between the two, missing. The lambs were calling things like, "Give my regards to the chef," and, "Well, at last, a decent orgy." I ignored their comments and acted as though what awaited them in the barn was much better than the pellets they had pigged out on. Jim even suggested I go back in the barn, pick the food up, and try again the next evening. Picking up four pounds of medicated food pellets is roughly equivalent to picking up four pounds of popcorn kernels. I suggested that once I got them back to the barn they could cool their hooves there if it took them two weeks to clean up the food.

After an hour of cajoling on my part, the lambs made it back to the barn and finished the food as though they hadn't had a thing to eat all day.

In that one brief evening the lambs had furthered my education and made me a better person. I learned never to trust an innocent lamb with a paper bag full of pellets. These ten sheep may have surpassed their genetic pool. For centuries Texas has produced billions of dumb sheep. Jim had to bring home ten lean Fulbright scholars.

Later on that summer, I went to a different feed store to buy the lambs' food because our neighbor said that this store might be cheaper than the one we had been going to. I went in to get two sacks. The other store never confused the issue when I bought feed: I'd say, "I'd like two bags of lamb pellets," and the kid would say, "Yes, Ma'm, will that be cash or charge?" then, "Where is your truck?" I'd write a check and never have to show identification; he'd carry the sacks to the pickup, and I'd be on my way.

I walked into this store and said, "I'd like two bags of lamb pellets," and the fellow asked, "What kind of sheep ya' got, lady?" I didn't want to boast too much about how precious they were or what beautiful eyes Charles Lamb had in his otherwise lopsided head, so I just stuck to the facts: "Well, they have four legs, two eyes, and one ear."

"No, no, no lady. Are they range sheep or show?"

I told him they just ate grass and weeds, minded their own business, and were not exhibitionists, so he sold me range pellets. The other feed was for fattening show stock. Discrimination is everywhere rampant. All sheep are equal but some are fatter than others.

As that first summer grew hotter, and the grass grew shorter, I would go to the field below the lambs' territory to pull cane for them at least once, and sometimes twice a day, depending upon the amount of noise they made. They were the ones considered the foraging animals, but I was the one out in the field sweating for them as they waited in the shade. I decided it must be more fun raising cane than pulling it.

In November of that first year, Jim rented a ram for our flock because he was taken by the notion that if ten sheep were good, fifteen would be better, and so on, on a yearly basis, until we owned millions, all grazing on five acres.

The ram was the ugliest father since the Victorian era, with muttonchop sideburns and a macho mien. The fee for his service was one dollar a ewe plus room and board. He ate high on Purina pellets, enjoyed dessert of ground alfalfa and molasses, and hung around two weeks. If that ram had known his take-home pay was only two dollars and fifty cents a week, he might not have been so arrogant.

In April our flock began its increase. Fortunately the first baby was born on a Sunday, and the last three during my spring break. I marvelled at the precise timing and told Jim that

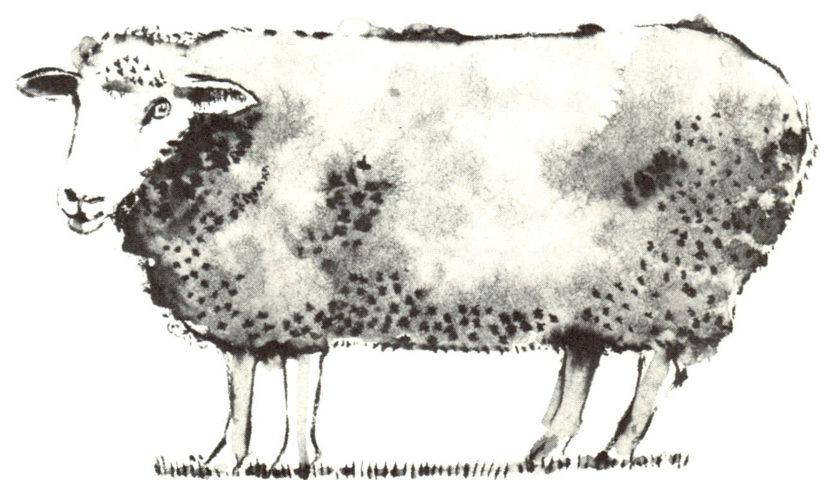

if it had not happened so conveniently, I might have had to take maternity leave. He said it wasn't really necessary to put pink or blue ribbons on the baby's neck and fresh flowers on the mother's nightstand.

(Actually, this is a good idea. It will keep you from thinking up nice names for all the babies. Without the ribbons, you'll find yourself saying to friends who visit, "And I want you to meet Charles Lamb, and Lamb Patty and Julie and Chuckie, . . ." because you name blue ribbons as well as pink. Save yourself a little heartbreak and name only pink ribbons, because eventually the blue ribbons disappear only to reappear in that great freezer chest in the garage.)

The first lamb was born in the driveway. The mother picked a little grassy spot next to the fence and delivered the baby within fifteen minutes of being let out of the barn. She picked a place without fire ants and out in the open. While she was cleaning the little lamb, she was cooing and crooning. In thirty minutes or so, when he looked like a white washboard, she began nudging him to his feet. First one set of legs would go up and then the other, then the first set would collapse, and he'd be sprawled over the grass. Eventually, he was up and leaning against his mother and within an hour trying to nurse. The ewe couldn't have picked a better day, or a better spot. The sun was out, which helped dry the lamb and allowed him to soak up plenty of warmth during his first hours.

Mid-morning, after walking a few feet and cooing, and going back to the baby and nudging it, the ewe managed to take the baby to the deeper grass in the orchard under a shade tree where they stayed until two in the afternoon. Jim told me to pick the lamb up and take it to the barn, but when I went out, the lamb was on his feet nursing, and the mother walked the baby all the way to the barn. She stopped a time or two and the lamb would lean against her, but the baby made it from the drive in the orchard to the barn which was a pretty good walk for an eight-hour old baby.

The little lamb was all pink and white and had the loveliest, most symmetrical ears imaginable—they looked like bleached schefflera leaves.

While the lambs were lounging around in the orchard, Jim and I fixed up the maternity suite in the barn. We took a gate off a stall in the old barn and put it on the end stall of the lamb's barn to make a secure place for the new baby. Then we put down fresh hay for the floor and put in a supply of food and a pail of water. We kept the mother and lamb in there the rest of Sunday and all day Monday. By Tuesday, Jim opened the barn and allowed them to graze in the field after the other lambs went to the orchard. The two had it all to themselves until the baby, who was born inquisitive, crawled through the gate and was separated from his mother who tried to butt the gate down to get to her little one. Jim opened the gate to let the mother out, figuring if the baby was strong enough to crawl through a fence he was strong enough to socialize with the rest of the flock.

By this time, Bird had seen the new kid in town and took exception to his being here. Bird went over to let the kid know who was boss dog, and was attacked by two mothers. Then Jim swatted Bird with his cap, and for the final insult put her in the house to repent her sins.

That evening while we ate supper, the second baby was born. Since it was time for them to be put in the barn, I got a towel and picked the little thing up, but the mother was having none of that. The lambs like to clean their babies at the spot where they are born and get them on their feet at their own convenience, and if you mess around with that arrangement, you stand a chance of the mother's rejecting the baby.

Chester, our experienced shepherd-neighbor, came over and said to leave the lamb on the ground until the mother finished with it, then "walk" it back to the barn and the mother would follow.

We sat by the fence for the next hour listening to the ewe's song and watching the tiny shivering thing get to its feet, try to nurse, and fall flat on its face. Jim was concerned that the mother didn't have enough milk, but, finally, when the baby realized that the mother's knee wasn't the Source, it nursed for a few seconds.

By then, it was getting dark and Jim wanted to get them to the barn. I picked the baby up, again showed it to the mother, and started backing toward the barn while the mother started backing in the opposite direction. After much cooing on my part, and much foot-stomping on the ewe's part, Chester came back, took the lamb, held it at ground level so that its legs touched the grass, and "baahed" the ewe right into the maternity section.

The next morning I took a pail of warm water to the newest mother, and found that a third baby had been born overnight. After the other sheep left the barn, I closed the gate leaving the three mothers with their three babies inside, so that all the new mothers could stay in out of the damp weather.

Each stall was covered with fresh hay on the floor and fresh water in the pails. It looked better than our house. In fact, hay on the floor seemed to be a marvelous way to combat Plaster Dust and its cousin, Sand.

Because the second lamb born looked so tiny, Jim told me to buy a bottle and supplement for the little one. The supplement came in powder form, which you mix with warm water and test on your wrist. We mixed, and tested, and the babies—all three—said, "Yuck, I'd rather have my mother's knee than that stuff." Chester said that if a lamb were starving it would drink with relish. No one seemed to be starving.

Jim, during his "Now-let's-think-about-the-future" talk, decided that with the extra trap planted in grain, plus the garden acre the lambs could clean up after his harvest, he could support a herd of twenty-five. Support was right —if I could get a summer job.

I didn't know where the national economy was going, but I knew where ours was going: to the dogs, to the cats, to the sheep, to the armadillos. . . .

Gloria Rockem, the liberated cat who wore Bella Abzug hats and a little gold necklace with the letters "ERA" outlined in rhinestones, had three babies: two white ones and a calico.

Gloria looked as though she had been eating lemons one evening all stretched out on the top of the wood pile. The next evening she didn't show for supper. The morning after that she didn't show for breakfast. I walked through both barns figuring she had the kittens under the floor and found nothing, but heard little voices as soon as I turned on the lights in the garage. She had had three babies in the corner of the garage behind two sacks of concrete—a good enough barrier for Bird. Unless we opened one of the doors, Bird couldn't get into the garage and just stood outside the closed doors and breathed heavily. Gloria allowed me to pick up the kittens and put them in a clothes basket filled with straw covered with a beach towel. We put a sign out front:

RARE, Limited-Edition TFC* kittens. Only three left, to select home. Inquire within. Free delivery within one hundred miles.
*TFC - Texas Farm Cat.

There were no takers. We own four cats. (See page 41.)

Four days after the kittens were born, twin lambs were born early in the morning. After clearing the barn of everyone else, I moved the mother and babies to the maternity stall, and got her settled for the next few days. One lamb was tiny, and the other looked like Tarzana. All morning Tarzana nursed, and the tiny male just kept getting tinier. Jim and I cornered the mother and tried to get the runt to nurse, but found no milk on the mother's part, and lethargy on the baby's.

I tried the new formula from the feed store, but the hole in the nipple wasn't large enough, and the baby showed no interest in what little did trickle out. When the twins were about six hours old, the little one just leaned against the barn and counted his ribs. There was never a chance to nurse because Tarzana was there first. When Chester came over we tried the mother again, but were unable to squeeze a drop of milk out. Chester suggested using canned milk—the little ones prefer it. I mixed up a half cup of Carnation for each, and for the first time the runt actually moved his mouth. The end of the nipple looked like the recipient of a shotgun blast; it had so many needle holes that all the lamb had to do was swallow—the flow of milk was automatic if the bottle were turned upside down. Chester said they needed to be fed every three hours since the mother's supply was scarce or nonexistent.

By their third feeding the twins couldn't tell me from their real mother; we both smelled the same. No mother lamb will ever be mistaken for a bottle of Oscar de la Renta. By three in the afternoon, I decided I'd either have to shower and disinfect my clothes or move to the barn.

About noon, when I was feeding one baby, I heard that distinctive mother's song and across the field the last mother had had her lamb. It seemed fine and the ewe tended to it and had all afternoon to get it on its feet. The second mother got the stall next to the twins—just the same accommodations, except the door was a sheet of plywood and I had to climb over the fence to get to the feed box and water bucket.

Tarzana, re-named Lamb Patty, nursed for the first few hours when there was a questionable milk supply; after she took to the bottle, the ewe took over the care and feeding of the runt, and that was the way it remained. Either the ewe's milk hadn't arrived with the twins, or she just wasn't interested in raising two kids; Chester tried to milk her, I tried ("Ah-ha-ha-ha . . .," said Jim), and finally, several days later, Jim tried. That last day we had the ewe down, I tried one teat and got nothing, Jim tried the other and got a stream of milk that wet his coverall's leg and dripped into his shoe.

When it was feeding time, and we approached the lambs, Lamb Patty would come running to us, never looking back at the others. She loved her bottle, and tolerated Bird; however, I suspected she had a little memory bank that stored things like: "Bird butted me away from my bottle three times today," or "Bird got rough and chased my tail twice," and would recall them when she weighed a hundred pounds and had hard hooves.

By the end of the week, the barn smelled so outrageous that we decided to clean it out and spray for flies. All the babies were here, and the mothers were out of the maternity suite. We burned the top layer of straw and put the smaller pieces of straw and manure near the pecan trees in the back yard. There was a low place that was filled in with the plaster dust from the house that nothing would grow on until we put dirt over it. Lamb manure would certainly encourage something to grow if only another bull nettle.

The next week, we had a little problem with names during the shearing. When Jim bought the lambs, he knew for a fact that his purchase included five ewes, and their little ones—all of whom he believed to be female. Of course, later we realized that Charles Lamb was not, and named him accordingly. Then Charleen Lamb, who was so precious, so loving, so charming, so simpatico, was sheared and was known from that day forward as Chuckie. That was not the only surprise—there were three young muttons and only two females in that group of five young ones.

Jim and I had decided earlier to keep only females because males tend to meanness and could be dangerous if one ever decided to knock Jim's good leg out from under him. We had to do some rethinking about muttons (which has a curiously culinary sound about it, giving their short life specific direction) because a rose is a rose no matter what his gender. If Chuckie were smart enough to play ewe in drag for a year, then he was smart enough to be precious all his life and promise never to butt anyone.

He did lead a welcome movement to improve our garbage disposal. Vegetable trimmings and stale bread now go to the sheep. Chuckie especially loves onion peels, watermelon and cantaloupe rinds run a close second, and cabbage leaves are dessert.

The sheep shearing was the first I had ever seen. From the time the professional shearers cornered a lamb in the pen, dragged it out by its leg and nape of the neck, cut the wool off the legs, tied the legs together, sheared the body, head, and neck, untied the sheep, and went for another—barely five minutes elapsed. The sheep *looked* as though they'd had a five-minute hair-styling but none was badly maimed.

The power unit for the clippers was mounted on a trailer pulled by a pickup, and the two brothers set up their clipping rig on the ground in

back of the trailer. A stand that looked like an oil derrick without the Exxon logo was set up away from the truck and the big wool sack was dropped into the middle and cuffed over the top just like a Hefty-lined trash can, seven feet tall. On the side of this derrick was a small ladder. As each sheep was sheared, the wool was gathered in a large, number three washtub by the twelve-year-old son of one of the shearers. He would climb the ladder and dump the wool over the top into the sack. One time the little boy climbed up the ladder without a tub and jumped into the sack himself. That was called "compacting the wool."

If that dive into the wool sack didn't take the kid's breath away, it did his mother's. I'll bet no Cheer representative ever asked *her* to bring in dirty T-shirts for a brightness test.

We had a wool sack filled with one hundred and four pounds of wool from our ten sheep when the shearers were finished. No wonder the lambs were panting during the summer. They looked like white sponges without their dirty wool, but even the sparse wool that was left on their bodies was as oily as the long stuff was.

A week after shearing, Chuck was in danger of being put up for adoption with the local butcher, and the innocent lamb hadn't done a thing. The year-old lambs were running in the south trap, around the house and in the orchard, separated from the mothers and new babies. They had just been allowed back in that area after having been kept out during the two weeks the fence was being built.

Jim was happy to have them back since the grass was getting deep. His love of nature is pretty evenly divided between the lambs and his fruit trees. So, understanding the lambs' perfidious nature and accepting it, he took off several days from rasping wood and grappling with Liquid Nail to make cages for his beloved fruit trees—twenty-one new ones in all. He dug trenches, staked the cages, and opened the gates for the lambs, resting easy in the knowledge that his lambs were safe with the nice new fence, and his fruit trees were all safely caged.

Until he noticed his cages listing, then the leaves on the tree tops missing. Observing the trees frequently during the day, he found three of the lambs, the Fruit Tree Gang, using the cages for a foothold to get to the top of the trees. He tried gently shooing them away. Then he sent Bird in (warily, very warily. She remembered who rolled her three times before she knew what hit her). A day or so later, the lambs had bent and dented his cages so miserably that Jim was threatening to shoot them on the spot. He kept saying, "Those Goddamn lambs are going to be sold tomorrow."

Charles Lamb was the leader. "Spooky Male," as Jim referred to him, was another, and that "Long-Legged Bitch" was the third offender. I kept telling Jim that Chuck wasn't the cage climber, and he kept saying, "Well, he's the other male." Jim had a hard time understanding gender after the shearing trauma, and he didn't realize there were three males in the group and Chuck was home studying Interior Design while Charles and Spooky and Bitchy were doing the peach and plum trees in.

Jim was so protective of his fruit trees that he got his air pistol out to pop the lambs, misfired and blasted a hole in a new gallon container of Wisk, releasing enough soap in the shop file cabinet to wash down the Abscam papers.

Eventually, Jim added another two-foot band of wire to the tops of the cages. And eventually —inevitably—two of the Fruit Tree Gang (the muttons) went to market which lessened my appetite for choice lamb, but the young ewe's appetite hasn't lessened one iota for apple tree leaves.

If the time Jim spends tending his trees—fertilizing, digging trenches, making and remaking cages, and fending off the hungry hoards—were translated into minimum wages, we could have Fruit-of-the-Month delivered to our back door and have enough money left over for imported cheeses. But the challenge wouldn't be the same.

5

Materials

SINCE THE OLD HOUSE was de-walled by the Indians in 1888, Portland cement was born, and no one knows what lime mortar is, or checks the barn to see how much hair was shed by his horse to make hair plaster. No self-respecting concrete man mixes straw and mud anymore, either.

All old wood—trim and floors—is virtually knot free. There are so many small, tasteful knots in the new pine flooring that before you flip on the light switch, the pattern appears to be a roach convention.

When redoing an old house you will eventually have to come to grips with new materials. At least know what's available, and what's not available.

What's Not Available: Wood as thick as it used to be. There will be many times that you will have to improvise; it helps to have a creative genius on your team who solves three problems for every new one that comes up.

He will look at the new trim that doesn't cover the wallboard and isn't wide enough for door jamb, and either rip a board and rout it to match, or buy a piece of new door jamb, a piece of wood lathe, tack them together with little brass nails, and produce a finished trim that is as thick as trim used to be. This leaves a small seam on top of the trim that is not noticeable when the trim is painted. Custom-made trim is also nice, but you need to decide whether the production time involved is worth the effort.

What Is Available: Wood filler, caulk, insulation, Sheetrock, and peachy-keen tools.

WOOD FILLER

It is not possible to restore a house without an array of wood fillers at your disposal. Wood filler is to the restorer what catsup is to McDonald's: indispensable. There are several different kinds on the market, and many uses for each.

1. Weldwood: This filler is alcohol soluble. It becomes as hard as wood and can be treated like wood when it dries. The biggest drawback is

that it becomes hard and brittle; if it shrinks enough, it will not stay put. Weldwood works well in knotholes, and is used to smooth out cracks in furniture or woodwork, but was not designed for floors.

2. Paste Wood Filler: The Sherwin-Williams Paste Wood Filler can says that this filler was also not designed for floors. What do they know? A professional restorer recommended it, and it worked. It was, in fact, the only product that I could find (besides rope) that would do the job of filling in the cracks in the old flooring. Paste wood filler is also essential around door facings at floor level. This filler is thinned with mineral spirits.

3. H. Behlen and Brothers Paste Wood Compound: This filler comes in a small container and appears to be hard and solid, but can be scraped off with a putty knife and worked into cracks and crevices easily. After it dries, it has the feel of Weldwood without the shrinkage, and takes stain well. This filler is water soluble.

CAULK

1. Acrylic Caulk: Acrylic caulk is one of mankind's new miracle materials with the usual miracle material side effects.

Acrylic caulk is fun to apply. Put the caulk gun in one hand, a wet rag in the other, and you are in business. Use acrylic to caulk the perimeter of the ceiling, cracks in a wall, between boards, and around window and door frames. It will eventually crack, despite the literature on the subject to the contrary, but later on you can recaulk and your walls and windows will be in pretty good shape.

Never put acrylic caulk on the floor. Never caulk the base of a commode or the pedestal sink with acrylic. Acrylic caulk looks beautiful on the base of these fixtures and white tile—for maybe fifteen, twenty minutes. Then as it dries, magnetic properties come into play, and forever after there is constant movement on the floor. Dog hairs, dust bunnies, plaster dust, and crud gravitate toward this magnetic field twenty-four hours a day, especially during the night. Every morning after your pedestal sink is grouted with acrylic caulk, you can expect to see a black, furry collar around its base. Ditto the commode.

I researched the perfect solvent to remove the caulk. Razor blades took up slivers, sheets, and hunks, but left residue. The residue took up dirt from shoes like bubble gum and still maintained that magnetic attraction for dog hair, dust bunnies, plaster dust, and crud. Paint remover turned it orange but did not in any way keep the caulk from doing its thing. Paint thinner and fingernail polish remover held possibilities, but even they were not effective. The literature fails in this area. No one is going to give you the REAL acrylic story. You are getting it here: once acrylic, always acrylic; take necessary precautions to keep it off the tile.

2. Spirit-Based Caulk: Cheap. Much cheaper

than acrylic caulk and more difficult to apply (by the time you finish a tube, your hands are covered with spiderweb-like strings), but a very effective caulk. When you have pulled yourself up from the morass of webs, cleaned your hands and the putty knife (which will pull threads and get as messed up as your hands), you can look at it more objectively; the caulk does seem to be less apt to crack than acrylic.

If cleanliness is a factor (the newly-plastered wall area around a window frame, for example), use acrylic caulk because any indiscretion can be wiped off the plaster with a wet rag before the caulk dries.

If what you're caulking is to be painted or covered up (the perimeter of a floor that will be trimmed with baseboard and shoe mold), go with the mineral-based caulk.

3. Cement Caulk: Cement caulk can be spirit-based or acrylic. Spirit-based cement caulk has the difficult properties of the cheaper caulk and the color and gritty texture of cement. It does a fine job of sealing cracks between a stone wall and an interior wood wall.

The acrylic cement caulk seems heavier than regular acrylic caulk designed for windows and doors and also does a fine job of binding together two different materials such as Sheetrock and plaster.

4. Clear Outside Spirit-Based Caulk: This is a fine caulk that seeks a level of smoothness as it dries, remains flexible and elastic, will not crack, and is unaffected by extremes in temperature. It is expensive. If you're dealing with a critical area that might rain on your inside parade if it is not watertight, float a loan. Some brands will run as high as six dollars a tube. Don't skimp.

5. Silicone Caulk That Nothing Sticks To: Caulk used by plumbers to fill cutoff pipes that will not be reused and that cannot be removed; or outside openings with smaller pipes threaded through them. *Nothing sticks to silicone.* If you're filling a cutoff pipe in the bedroom with the intention of plastering the area, be sure to push the silicone far back into the pipe so that your plaster will be able to catch the pipe and have something to hold on to.

CAULK GUNS

When buying a caulk gun (and you can't restore a doghouse without one) be very careful about the kind you buy.

In my ignorance, I thought there was only one kind: the kind that works for five or ten years, then gives up the ghost. Actually there are two kinds: the kind that works for five or ten years and then gives up the ghost, and the one that doesn't work at all—not even with the first tube of caulk.

All caulk guns look alike: they are painted surplus gunmetal grey or green and look like a ray gun. The long part is for the caulk tube and the trigger operates the plunger—unless, of course, you buy the wrong one and then 97 percent of the time nothing operates the plunger.

The right one looks like this:

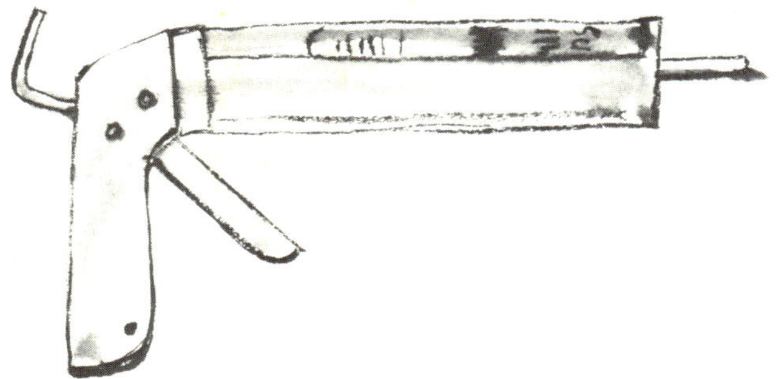

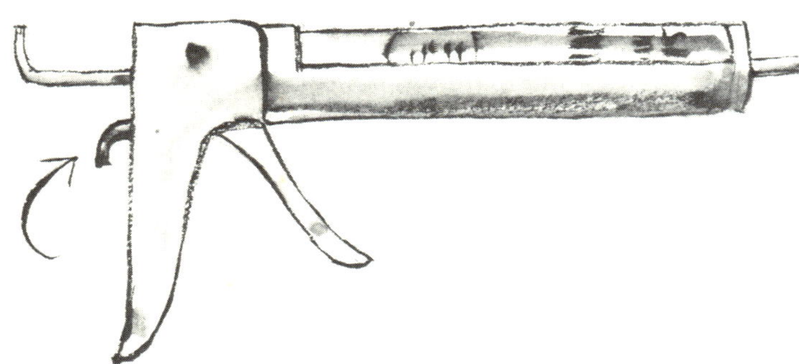

The wrong one looks like this and doesn't work at all. The plunger will push the bottom of the tube in such a manner that the caulk will seep out around it and by the middle of the tube will lack enough pressure to push the caulk out the nozzle. You will have to finish the tube by removing the contents from the bottom with a spatula, and if you have only one spatula and the cook is icing a cake with it, there will be domestic disharmony as well as disenchantment with the hardware salesman who pushed the lemon on you.

To Open the Caulk Tube: Use a sharp knife to cut the tip of the caulk nozzle at a slant. An old hat-pin (antique buffs will have several in the top bureau drawer) does a fine job of opening the inner membrane that releases the caulk. A coat hanger wire will do, but the nozzle opening will be larger, forever after releasing a thick stream of caulk even when you need only a tiny bead.

INSULATION

1. Fiberglass: Fiberglass insulation is of prime importance if you plan to winter in your newly-restored home. Fiberglass bats were not around a hundred years ago, so don't expect to find any in the attic. But don't hesitate to put some there yourself, even if it isn't authentic. No one will ever know it's there if you don't tell them. You put the fluffy part up, and the foil back down so that your attic, in its dimness, looks like a pink carpeted spaceship afloat in a black hole.

The bats are awkward, but not so heavy that they can't be managed by the middle-aged restorer. The biggest drawback to laying insulation is the fiberglass itself, which will turn your skin pink and your lungs to hamburger. Wear a face mask (available at most lumber yards, hardware stores, or Woodcraft), long sleeves, and a tight collar. Thin gloves will protect your hands.

2. Polystyrene: Polystyrene comes in panels the same building size as Sheetrock, but hauling a 4 x 8 board to your attic may present a problem. This seems to be used more in new wall construction and, if your house is frame, it wouldn't be practical to rip off siding; however, if you are making inside shutters for your windows, you can cover this rigid insulation with fabric (or wood veneer, for that matter), slip the panel in a frame, and hang at your window for an energy-saving device.

3. Sprayed Foam (Urea-Formaldehyde and Urethane): Sprayed foam, which is as beautiful as hand-applied plaster, does not come up to building codes in some areas and has the added disadvantage of smelling bad. Not all sprayed foam leaks an odor, but you won't know for sure until it has been applied, and then it will be too late. Urea-formaldehyde has recently come under the gun because it causes cancer in laboratory animals. In addition to its assumed detrimental effect on humans, sometimes the foam will shrink, thereby diminishing its effectiveness as insulation. Either way, it seems to be bad news. You might be better off sticking with the more conventional insulations.

4. Dacron Bat: When you have the window trim removed and sent out to be stripped, you can fill the void between the rock walls and the window with Dacron bat, the same thing you use for quilts or to stuff soft toys. You can use scraps of quilt bat left over from quilting projects or, if you don't quilt, buy bags of the toy stuffing. It isn't very expensive and is easier and more comfortable to work with than fiberglass.

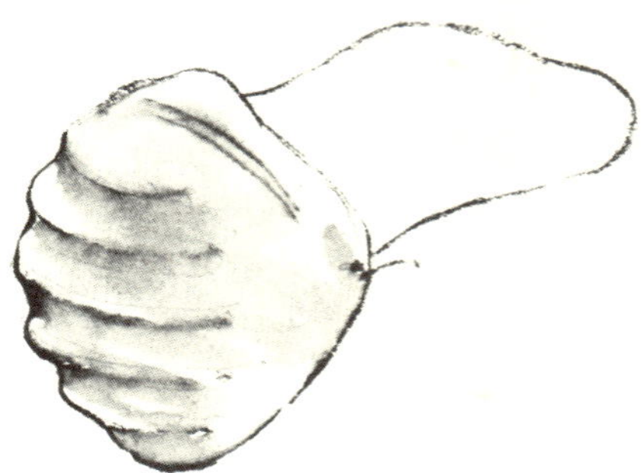

SHEETROCK

Unless you have wood lathe put back and plastered, or metal lathe installed and plastered at the same time the inside rock walls are being done, you'll almost have to confront the Sheetrock market.

On a ceiling, thin three-eighth inch Sheetrock can be used. If you have a heavily trafficked room, three-quarter inch for walls might be more practical, but if you're not given to losing your temper and kicking a wall or ramming your fist through the closet, one-half inch is just as good.

All Sheetrock, even the three-eighth inch stuff, is heavy and awkward if nailing overhead. Holding a sheet against wall studs and nailing it tight doesn't seem to be much of a problem, but balancing it overhead is quite another story.

Transporting Sheetrock more than thirty or forty inches is also another story. It will be contribution enough if you just buy the stuff at the lumberyard, bring it home in the pickup, and store it downstairs by pulling it through an open window.

Finishing the Sheetrock up to and including the tape-and-float portion is one of those jobs that can be done by a carpenter and helper for very little cash outlay (experienced men will be able to finish the job before the amateur can buy Sheetrock nails).

Taping calls for a degree of skill and dexterity (overhead dexterity if you're talking ceilings) that doesn't come with the purchase of a container of joint compound and a four-inch putty knife. Unless you have apprenticed yourself to a tape-and-float man, you stand a good chance of botching up a room or two before you get the hang of it.

You can safely texture and paint the Sheetrock. Buy the joint compound, or texture, premixed (first, use what's left over from the taping). The five gallon bucket is very heavy, but it will cover a lot of surface. You can buy powdered texture and mix it with water, but the premixed is not that much more expensive and is that much easier to use. You're going to need all the energy you can muster to texture the ceilings and walls with the roller. Premixed texture also comes in its own bucket; you don't have to look for a pan big enough to sauté an elk in order to mix up a batch.

Add water to the joint compound until it becomes the consistency of thick paint. Pour enough of this mixture in your paint tray to fill it half full. Use a fluffy paint roller and apply like paint (the fluffier the roller, the more visible the texture). You can put an extension handle on the paint roller and do the ceiling from the floor. Allow the texture to dry a day or two before applying paint.

PEACHY-KEEN TOOLS

For those restorers to whom money is no object, simply buy the best tool and its owner.

To the rest of us to whom money is not only an object but frequently only a figment, get the best tool you can afford and know how to use it.

Sanders: Belt and Vibrator

The restorer could use two sanders: the belt sander and a Rockwell orbital sander. The belt sander with a heavy grit belt will eat into wood if you let it get away from you. If you have a high place that needs to be leveled, the belt sander held with both hands—carefully—will do the job quickly. For the finish sanding, use the Rockwell sander with the appropriate grit sandpaper.

If you are finishing a piece of furniture, and want a buttery smooth finish, work from medium (120) to fine (220) to extra fine (320), which is only slightly less abrasive than your own hands.

Rasp/File

Get two rasps: one with a working surface from end to end, and another with an ash handle. Each rasp will have one curved side and one flat side; one coarse file surface, and a finer, smoother surface. The coarse surface will be used to cut down as much wood as you need to get rid of, and the finer surface will smooth rough edges.

Pinch Bars

Pinch bars remove mistakes—yours and some other restorer's. They effectively remove car-siding wainscoting that was put up seventy years ago, closets that were added fifty years ago, cabinets that were built over the rock wall twenty years ago, and the ceiling trim that you nailed upside down. You'll need two bars—one for you and one for your helper. The bars are also effective nail pullers that reach where claw hammers won't.

Nail Pullers

In addition to claw hammers and pinch bars, a nail-puller manufactured in France will frequently keep the air from turning blue. It will hang on to the tiniest shred of nail and yank it out even if its head has long since vanished. It will remove staples that have been used to secure foam padding to floors, and tacks. This is an essential tool if anything has to be removed before your restoration begins.

Skill Saw and its companion, the Speed Square

The first summer, I had such respect for the skill saw I wouldn't use it. I rationalized that since it was impossible to cut a straight line, it was of little or no use. Then Jim bought a gizmo called a Swanson Speed Square, which is, in reality, a triangle with a lip that catches the edge of your board and presents a raised edge to guide the saw in a straight line, making a straight cut and happy carpenters. The second summer I became proficient with the saw, but had no less respect for it. The secret to finger longevity is to ask yourself before pulling the trigger, "Do you know where your fingers are?" or, "Have you hugged your thumb today?"

A NOTE ON RESTORER'S GARB

The restorer's wardrobe is perhaps even simpler than Nancy Reagan's. The restorerette needs to stick to classic designs, basic, yet always in good taste. For tops, go for the polyester blend in work chambray, because it is carefree and will take you from the hardware store to the lumberyard to McDonald's with complete confidence.

True, you can buy the all natural, all cotton chambray at select boutiques (Sears and Penney's), but they do demand extra care that will cut into your busy life-style. You won't be able to find the ironing board most of the time, and when you do, the Olympic Stain that decorates the front of the shirt smells funny when pressed.

For slacks, Jordache is gauche—too obvious. Try the Junior League/Salvation Army shops which usually carry jeans that are just the correct shade of faded blue with textured hems—*de rigueur* for working in the grass burrs and bull nettles or dragging through the plaster dust.

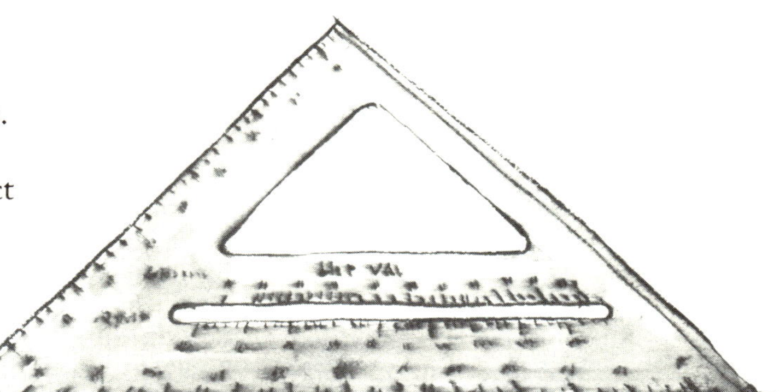

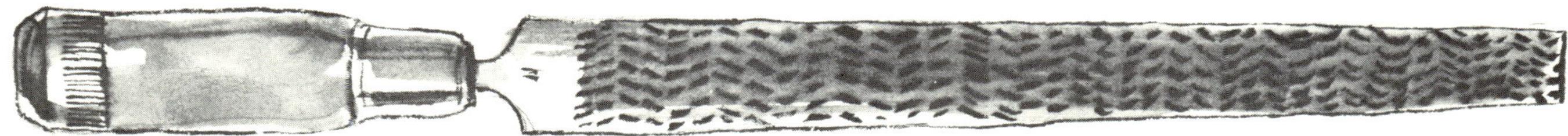

6
Climate Loosely Controlled

LONG BEFORE THE modern Trombe wall was invented as a way to capture solar energy, early Texas farmhouse builders were sticking their wet index fingers into the prevailing winds and orienting their houses on a north/south axis.

The trick was to bring the winter sun in and keep the summer sun out by overhangs, porches, and judicious planting.

The early builders put in large windows placed to catch the breeze, designed inside walls to allow cross ventilation, and made eleven-foot ceilings to facilitate cooling.

In the case of rock houses, the stone mass acted as a heat sink in winter, warming rooms without heat. During the hot summers, the stone mass retained the morning cool well into the afternoon. This old rock house still responds to weather as though it had its own thermostat.

Before we moved to the country, utility rates were escalating as rapidly as Jim's blood pressure. Jim took the rising cost of energy personally; his vendetta was directed at the oil producers. Our cars were VW's—as economical as we could go without pedaling—and had been for twenty years, but just to show that he didn't take gasoline waste lightly, Jim posted his WW II "Is This Trip Necessary?" signs in strategic places.

His real conservation thrust, however, was aimed at the utilities. The air conditioner was set on 82°. This wasn't too bad if you were sitting under the ceiling fan drinking iced tea in your Underoos, but if you actually had to move around (light dusting, or getting from living room to kitchen to freshen your tea), you could work up a little perspiration. Heavy labor (making beds, gathering trash, and vacuuming) called for a bandana round your head, and Scotch tape on the bridge of your bifocals. Living primitively does not generate more discomfort than Jim's idea of summer air conditioning in Texas at the prevailing rate.

The central heating system was fueled by natural gas, and Jim had no more inclination to feather the natural gas suppliers' nest than he had inclination to send City Public Service a bonus check at Christmas.

In winter, the thermostat was set at 62° and sealed with a drop of wax to make sure no one—BUT NO ONE—touched it. Not even a farmhouse without central heat is more uncomfortable than the city house at 62°. In order to circumvent the blue finger syndrome, we lived closely in the bedroom with the ceiling vents wide open, and the bathroom heater burning constantly. In a seven-room house, we lived in one, and still made the big CPS monthly payment.

As far as house lighting was concerned, Jim was ever vigilant. For a while I thought he was going to produce the Helen Keller story for South Texans, and Bird and Lili and I were being groomed for minor parts. Every time we got out of a chair and wandered into another room (the kitchen, for instance, for hot coffee, tea, or—if the fingers were too far gone—a mug of grog and a digitalis), Jim would yell, "Turn off those damned lights."

We learned to navigate the dining room, the butler's pantry, and find the kitchen that was dimly illuminated by a street light, within a month of the beginning of the energy crunch. Furniture rearranging was put on hold, and Bird and Lili would show fang if you approached either of their beds with the impish air of an interior decorator who has thought of a more exciting placement. Lili was getting old and said if she had to live in a cave like a bat, the least I could do would be to leave her bed alone.

Jim remembered the wood stove of his youth and the lovely heat generated by it with a few sticks of wood. Since the Texas Hill Country is always ten degrees cooler than San Antonio in the summer (and ten degrees colder in the winter), we decided to forego the pleasure of central air conditioning and central heat, and go primitive—ceiling fans, big windows, and an airtight wood-burning stove for the winter.

The first winter was miserable—the windows had not been replaced and the room we lived in had a hole in the north window covered with cardboard and plastic tape. The first summer was hotter than any summer had been for fifty years. Because we were so determined to break the air conditioning habit, we do not have many unpleasant memories from that summer except that afternoons were hard on Lili who has lupus and glaucoma and didn't need heat-stroke to complicate her life.

We kept her in her little bed, with wet towels draped over the foot of the big bed under the ceiling fan. If the rest of us were unduly uncomfortable we weren't aware of it because we were busy keeping her comfortable.

The second summer was lovely with no record-breaking heat waves. We learned to stay out of the midday sun, drink lots of iced tea, and if, for any reason, we had to work outside, Jim wore his good-ol'-boy cap, and I wore a straw hat with a large brim and always a long-sleeved shirt.

Jim, having been raised on a farm and in the open, considered the city confining, but not as much as a house with closed, shuttered windows. Living as we had was a double imprisonment for him, but a clean imprisonment.

When you go primitive, expect to live close to the earth; some of the earth will be on your living room floor, and the rest of it will be in your Oriental rugs. The civilized dust bunnies you left in the city turn into tumblebug bunnies in the country, and you will have to get used to traffic patterns on the floor.

You will feel clammy when the weather is damp but not cold enough for a fire, cold in unheated parts of your house on overcast days in the winter, and capable of working up a sweat in the summer when you're cooking a big roast for company (nothing new—except you can now stand in front of a window without getting claustrophobic).

If you stay with it long enough, however, you learn to go with the natural flow; buy two wool dust mops (one for upstairs and one for down), and a can of Sevin Dust for the tumblebugs. You will have company for barbecue in the summer, and save the roast turkey for the first norther.

SELECTION OF A WOOD STOVE

If you've decided to go rustic, buy a *good* wood stove. A cheap imitation of any brand will cost you money in the long run. Jøtul has a wide range of sizes to fit almost any amount of space you need to heat.

Vermont Castings has a reputation to match Jøtul, with the added advantage of having an open fire option without losing all of its efficiency. The Jøtul people, too, offer the open fire option in the Combi-1 and -6, but these are very modern looking and are not as compatible with an old house as the Vermont Castings' Defiant which looks like a Franklin stove, but with top-notch efficiency. (Vermont Castings also offers enamel.)

One of the most beautiful, and one that would fit in most graciously in a restored house, is the Woodstock. This one is made of soapstone, with ornate corners that hold the soapstone sides and top together.

Our first airtight wood-burning stove was the basic black Jøtul because I wasn't too crazy about the locally available color, an insipid green. After a year with the basic black, that green took on a new richness I couldn't live without. The second Jøtul, placed in the living room, was the enameled 118; it was well worth the extra money.

If I had it to do again, both stoves would be enamel if the only color available were purple, because the basic black is impossible to clean. When you pass a dust rag over its surface, you can kiss that rag goodby, or use it to get a dark, antique patina on your oak and pine pieces. The enameled stove is as easy to clean as dusting an enameled cast-iron dutch oven.

I have a friend who cannot understand my enamel stove preference. She says she cleans her black wood stove with the vacuum cleaner. I do not know what her floors look like.

The advantages of central heat are the convenience, the safety, and the total lack of involvement on your part. (I mean your immediate, personal involvement; your bank account will be plenty involved at bill-paying time.) It is easier to adjust a thermostat than haul in wood, and you can't smash a finger on a kilowatt hour.

With an airtight stove, bringing in wood is a problem; ash removal is another. An ash hopper helps with the latter problem: the lid keeps the ashes from pirouetting on a bucket handle, leaping into the air, and landing on your ceiling fan. Airborne ash is impossible to contain and the hopper nips this activity in the bud if you shovel the ash out slowly and deliberately. If you just dump a shovelful in a bucket, the particles will still be settling three days after you clean.

When transporting logs, use a large canvas

carrier and store the wood in a metal container by the stove.

Starting a fire is a problem until you learn the tricks of Boy Scouting. Initially, I followed the Brunarian Spiral: tiny to big; toothpicks to matches to wood slivers to kindling to lumber scraps to small oak logs to big oak logs. Usually, I'd progress through several stages only to have the fire quit on me and have to start all over again. Then I discovered that two large sheets of newspaper would start a nice fire; I could move right on up to kindling, and have a roaring fire in less than a minute with the help of one kitchen match.

There is a big difference between wood heat and central air, and the word for that difference is warmth; wood heat puts roses on your cheeks, dries out your furniture, and imparts a sense of fiscal calmness to your mind. You don't worry about the going rate of the kilowatt hour, nor care if the Arabs decant their oil in sterling vessels. The airtight stove keeps you warm for a long time on a cord of wood.

When installing the stove, use the thin-walled black stovepipe in the room itself (OK, OK. If the change in color from gross green to black hurts your sensibilities, check with your stove company and see if they can come up with an enameled pipe. If you have enough money, you can satisfy almost any whim.) This allows the heat that does go up the pipe to radiate into the room. You want double-walled, stainless steel, insulated pipe in the attic and through the roof. It is expensive, but you can't afford to be without it. Eat hamburger, plant a garden, or become a tour guide and charge strangers to see your house; but get good heavy insulated pipe for the attic because you can't be expected to crawl up through that trap door every evening after the news to check on attic fires.

Because wood heat dries the air completely, the first winter with the new heating arrangement found us living in an atmosphere straight out of the Sahara. The result was dry respiratory tracts, dogs with static electricity, and large cracks in our furniture.

The next winter I put a porcelain tea kettle filled with water on top of the Jøtul. It looked great, and only had to be refilled every couple of weeks. The dogs still sparked when you touched them, and the furniture still cracked.

Then the Cedar Swamp Steamer came along; it is the perfect companion to wood heat. It puts as much as a half gallon of moisture into the room daily. The doors of the kleidershrank no longer fly open when you walk past because they are no longer dry and shrunken. Bird's hair lies gracefully on her back without sparks shooting into the air when she rolls over, and our respiratory tracts are so well adjusted we no longer need blood transfusions by Valentine's Day.

The steamer is a two-part affair—a large bowl with a lid which has a hole in the middle that looks a little like a volcano. It is heat-resistant stoneware, subtly decorated, attractive, and very functional.

FIREWOOD

The fuel for your wood-burning stove is wood, which may not surprise you, although a few models can burn either wood or coal. Check the literature that comes with your stove. If it is not a switch-hitter, you could ruin the stove and burn your house down by using coal. Coal fires are much hotter and much dirtier than wood.

Order your wood by the cord and get a reputable wood seller to deliver it. High school kids are usually very dependable suppliers. Caveat emptor: One lady had been used to buying wood from a dealer who delivered and stacked the cord in a small tin building for her. After several years, the dealer vanished, and she had to buy from someone else. When the new cord was delivered and stacked, the tin building was full and there was still wood to be stored. She said to the new delivery man, "I can't understand it. A cord always fit before." A cord of wood will fill a four by four by eight-foot space no matter who delivers it.

When you order, you will be asked if you want green wood or cured. Cured wood is dry wood, and green is just cut; green wood needs to dry out for a season, while cured wood is ready to be burned. In a bind, you can burn green wood in an airtight stove, but it contains more moisture and burns slower than dry wood. Never burn green wood in a fireplace.

Never order wood—any kind of wood—in the summer unless you also have it stacked by someone else. One cord of wood stacked by you on a ninety-eight degree day in July weighs exactly three tons more than the same cord of wood stacked when the temperature is thirty-six degrees, and you will consume gallons of lemonade in order to finish the job. Just stick to ordering your wood at the end of winter when the temperatures are still nippy, and you can squirrel a cord away in the barn in less than an hour.

FEATHER BED - DOWN COMFORTER

A down comforter can be purchased by city and country dweller alike—old house enthusiast or modern purists. They are lovely no matter what your political persuasion but they are expensive, so more Republicans own down comforters, while Democrats own feather beds. They are gloriously warm, which is nice if the Jøtul that is lit is four rooms away and ice sheets are forming on the inside of your bedroom windows.

The comforters are generally available with channel quilting. Rather than just dumping two pounds of chicken feathers in a bag and sewing

up the opening, rows of channel-shaped pockets are created, and the feathers or down distributed equally among them. This is a better way than no pockets at all.

Another stitching configuration is the square. The comforter starts out with channels, then rows of stitching cross them at equal distances so that the comforter consists of square pockets of down. This is a marvelous way to do business, because the comforter will never be pear-shaped. However, it has been written that each line of stitching in a down comforter releases heat and trapped warmth, and causes the comforter to be less effective than the one with fewer seams. You pay your money and you take your pick.

There are a number of places that sell down comforters, and the prices vary as widely as the geographical locations. We ordered ours from Eddie Bauer's who offered channel-sewn comforters in gold/yellow or blue/light blue. The newest catalog offers cream which is the only color to buy. You need a cover for the comforter and if the comforter cover is a light solid, the yellow/gold or blue/light blue will show through.

Color, however, isn't as important as weight. Eddie Bauer has two—arctic weight and summer weight. Of course, right away you know Eddie Bauer lives up north, because while Texas winters may sometimes be indistinguishable from the arctic, no one ever needs a down comforter in the summer. If you scratch the fancy adjectives, you can buy one big, heavy comforter, and a lighter one, and be set for fall, winter, and spring.

At the onset of winter, the big comforter is too hot, and the dogs can't tolerate it. Use the lightweight one and everyone is comfy. Later on with the ice sheets on the windows, put the heavy one on the bed, fold the light one in two and put it on the foot of the bed, and you are ready for the big 0.

Size is also a consideration. I have always believed that if large is good, bigger is better, so I ordered a queen-size for a double bed, which was a mistake. When you make up the bed in the morning, you need to "fluff" the comforter in order to distribute the down. The only way to do this is to hold it at the fat end (at the foot—that's where the feathers migrate overnight) and flip it. All the pictures in the catalogs show a ninety-eight pound body holding onto an airborne comforter which is getting ready to settle squarely on the bed with equal overhang to the right and to the left. When I get the forty-ounce job airborne, it drops to the floor, completely clearing the bed. You are going to have to resolve this problem the best you can; you can either ask for help, or simply drag it off the floor onto the bed.

The comforter looks smashing and is easier to handle without the cover, but unless you own a miniature poodle who has cream-colored hair that absolutely does not shed, and a nose that does not drip (or eyes that do not water), you'd better have a cover for your comforter.

You can save again by buying two sheets (to match or contrast with your own bed linens), and make your own cover. Even the least skilled needle person should be able to whip one up in no time. Get the measurements of your comforter—Eddie Bauer's double-bed size is 81 x 86—and subtract one inch in each direction so that the finished case would be 80 x 85. This assures a nice compact fit. Sew the two sheets together like a big pillowcase. Put four or five ties at the closed end—inside the sack—and sew ties spaced to match the cover on the comforter itself. (Caution: When sewing the ties on the comforter, be very careful to sew through the piping or trim only, and not through the fabric that keeps the down at bay—otherwise you will have feathers migrate right out of the comforter and fill the cover, which is not what you want.)

Tie them together, pull the sack over the comforter and mark the end flap which will be closed with Velcro. (You could make buttonholes and sew on little pearl buttons, but then you'd hear the little buttons hit the iron bedstead and risk waking Bird in the middle of the night.)

If you really want to go country, you could whip up a quilt top—either pieced or appliqued—and use it for the top of your comforter sack.

INSULATED CURTAINS

In the summer in an old restored house, less is better: clean windows without curtains. In the winter, unless you have triple glazed windows that are tight and snug, glass will rob the heat from your room as surely as though you opened a door.

Make insulated tab curtains for all your windows for the winter. During the day, when the sun is out, push the curtains back and let the sun do its thing. At night, the insulated curtains will keep the cold out and keep the warm air in the room, not condensing on your window panes.

Use a smooth percale sheet for the top, a less expensive muslin sheet for the back. (Always use a white or off-white lining no matter what color you choose for the front of the curtain; that way all your windows will be uniform from the outside.) A flannel sheet-blanket will do nicely for the insulation. Buy one extra top sheet for tabs and facings.

1. Wash all sheets before doing anything. When you have finished, these curtains will be as washable as your bed linens.

2. Take the extra percale sheet and rip strips of fabric 4½ inches wide, fold in half and stitch. Cut the tabs 5½ inches long and turn right side out. If you have a machine that makes fancy stitches, the tabs look nice embroidered on both sides, and the extra stitching makes a stronger, more substantial hanger for the curtains.

3. Cut off selvage on both sheets and flannel sheet-blanket.

4. Rip the top edge off the percale and muslin sheets.

5. Clip the edge and pull a thread across the flannel sheet-blanket; cut along this line for a straight, true edge. You could rip the flannel but it's a big mess and just easier to pull a thread and cut.

6. Match the top percale sheet to the flannel insulation so that these two pieces are the same size. The Sears percale and flannel are compatible which makes the measuring and fitting easier.

7. Measure the width of the percale/flannel piece and cut or rip the muslin sheet 4″ narrower. (You might even want to buy a smaller muslin sheet to save wasting material. You could buy a twin percale, a twin flannel, and a "cot" muslin which is several inches smaller, and needs only the selvage trimmed.)

8. Sew the muslin sheet to the percale/flannel piece at the sides. Turn to the outside.

9. Rip a piece of muslin 4″ wide and 2″ longer than the curtain is wide for the top facing.

10. Place finished tabs evenly spaced along the top (9 tabs will be enough for a twin sheet curtain, and 12 for a full sheet curtain) and cover with facing. Sew through all thicknesses.

11. Turn facing, tuck end under, and whip down by hand.

12. Hang the curtain for a week or more before taking the hem. This gives the flannel and percale a chance to get to know one another.

13. Rip off all but 6″ excess fabric.

14. Mark curtain with chalk at floor level. Turn the percale/flannel piece as one and whip by hand. If the 6″ percale/flannel hem seems bulky, cut off the flannel layer at the floor and sew percale hem to the flannel. Baste the lining hem as a continuation of the front; the bottom of the curtain should have a hem similar to a pillowcase hem, but with a thicker front. Be sure to hem as close to the floor as you can. The curtain should brush against the floor but not drag.

This curtain will go a long way to make life more comfortable in a drafty old house.

If these instructions are less than crystal clear, write to me in care of the publisher and I'll try to provide more detail. Don't be bashful. The most personal mail I get is a Horchow catalog; I wouldn't mind getting requests from real people and writing a few notes.

You can buy wooden curtain rod sets at any department store that sells curtain hardware, but the ones that jut out any distance from the wall are useless. The insulated curtain would hang free of the window and allow as much cold in and heat out as Irish lace.

Cohasset sells a tab curtain rod of maple that is well made and inexpensive. However, if the window is medium size to large, the maple dowels will sag.

A better bet is to make your own if you have a jig saw or band saw and a good ripping saw of some kind.

1. Using the pattern, cut out two brackets

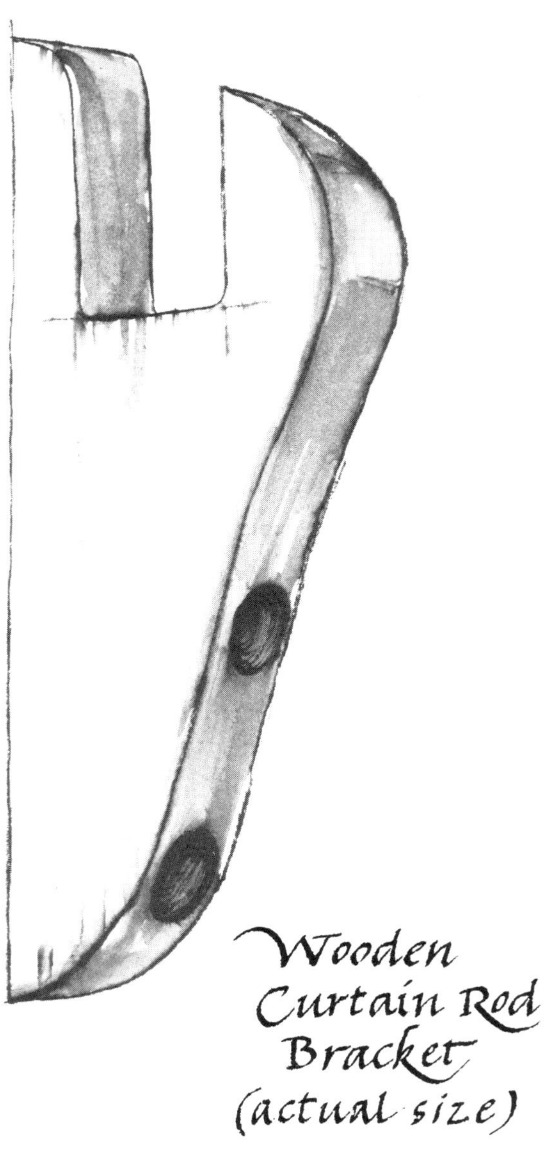
Wooden Curtain Rod Bracket (actual size)

for each window. This setup will accommodate itself to windows at least 50″ wide. (The maple dowels will warp spanning a space as narrow as 32″.) The pattern fits a window with a 5″ facing. You may have to adjust the length—either shorten it, or add a little if you want the bracket to fit the width of your facing neatly.

2. Drill and countersink holes in each bracket as indicated.

3. Rip the maple board at 1″ intervals for the curtain rods. If the opening is wider than 50″, it would be a good idea to enlarge the rod to 1¼ or 1⅜ and adjust the bracket accordingly.

4. Cut rods to length, sand, and stain.

If you use fine sandpaper and leave the maple feeling like cold butter, it won't take any kind of stain; but if you use a medium-grit sandpaper first, then sand the curtain rod just enough so that it is smooth to the touch but still a little roughed up, it will take enough of the Cohasset stain to blend in with one-hundred-year-old wood. The smoother job always looks like new wood.

Do not economize and use pine. Maple, ash, or cherry are all strong woods that can be stained to match anything. Cherry would just need a coat of tung oil before hanging.

INTERIOR SHUTTERS

In the summer, the uncurtained open windows in the farmhouse are wonderful until your eyesight begins to dim because of the glare at high noon. The heat will reflect off the white gravel drive into the kitchen window and raise inside temperatures (and tempers) considerably. You need to cut out glare and cut down light, but you do not need to diminish air flow.

With double-hung windows, you may want to install louvered shutters that cut glare in the summer and act as insulation in the winter (under the insulated curtains). Sears offers one of the largest selections of finished or unfinished shutters in louvered or fabric-insert style. The louvered shutters can control air flow, reduce glare, and make a boxcar look like a house from *Architectural Digest*.

The insert shutter is lovely, but not as versatile as the louvered. The fabric-insert shutter is useless as far as summer glare is concerned. If the window is open, and the shutter is closed, you are not getting a breeze in your house. With the window and shutter open, you are getting breeze and glare. There is no middle ground with insert shutters.

If your windows are French windows that open into the room, shutters mounted on each side of the window will not be possible because you will be unable to open the window and close the shutter at the same time. The summer alternative in this instance is a free-standing screen made of large, louvered shutters hinged together, or an owner-made screen with lattice inserts (much less expensive than shutters, and very effective).

You can buy a lightweight ready-made lattice screen which costs less than fifty dollars and is attractive; but, unfortunately, so flimsy it can be blown over by a vigorous gust of wind.

To make your own screen, buy 1″ x 12″ lumber and rip into boards 2″ wide. Use these strips to make a shadow box frame for the wood lattice. Cut the 4′ x 8′ sheet of lattice into two or three equal panels. Secure the sized panels with small trim—front and back. Most inside screens are 17″ to 24″ wide and 66″ to 72″ high. Vary these dimensions until you get the right size for your windows.

Next, decide on a hinging pattern. Do you want the center panel projecting toward the room with the side panels folding back, or the central panel close to the window with side panels folding forward, or do you want to use the conventional accordion fold? You might want four panels instead of three, or five. Your window dimensions will determine size and number of panels.

The reversible hinges found on ready-made screens are too light for the shadow-box type frame. Use cabinet door hinges, but decide on the folding pattern *before* installing hinges. With one-way hinges, you won't have a choice once the screen is put together.

The lattice screens look cool and reduce glare. We kept our screens natural—which is to say, light. If they were painted a dark color, the contrast between the blinding glare and the dark lattice would be uncomfortable.

CEILING FANS

Ceiling fans were cooling Texans a long time before air conditioners. They were twirling around in high school auditoriums, general stores, and beer gardens, doing a fair to middling job of making life bearable. Then air conditioning was invented and the Joske's department store of my youth kept the thermostat at 62°. Walking into the store in July was a treat, but walking out was a brickbat in the face.

Next, mass air conditioning hit the market and everyone had to have a piece of the action. New houses were cooled, old houses were cooled, movie theaters, churches, and all businesses worth their salt were air conditioned. Houses and apartments were built helter-skelter without regard to nature, and the oil drain began in earnest.

Because some people still have to pull on suit jackets during the summer and put in a 9-to-5, it would not be practical to outlaw air conditioning. It does, however, seem unnatural to impose it on a building that was never meant to wear a condenser in the first place, if that building hasn't been penned in by a big city.

Ceiling fans come in several sizes and many finishes. You can buy enameled ones and brass plated ones; you can buy fans with light fixtures and fans without. Dream up your own combination and it will be available to you. If the new ones don't suit you, there are even shops that specialize in reconditioned antique fans.

The new Hunter ceiling fans come in thirty-six- and fifty-two-inch size with two-speed motors and an option that reverses the blades to bring warm air down from the ceiling in the winter.

We have Hunter fans, six of them, and they are magnificent. We do not have the reverse option; a friend does and feels it is not worth the extra money. The blades are noisy and vibrate excessively. This may be due to faulty installation (the serviceman who installed them has been back twice, but they still shimmy), or it may be the nature of the reverse mechanism. In either case, it isn't absolutely necessary to have the reverse in order to use the fans in winter. The low speed will keep the air moving.

Concerning installation: You need to have the heavy-duty cross-bracing, of course. (See page 75) You also need to have someone install it who knows what he's doing. You don't want to be eating your supper and find a forty-five pound Hunter motor in your soup bowl. If you don't know how to cross-brace and install the hook these fans hang on, call your electrician. A fan motor falling on your head is not a fan motor doing its job.

ATTIC FANS

Old houses were designed to allow free circulation of air—heated air from a fireplace or stove in the winter, and fresh air in the summer. The attic fan cools an old house with high ceilings more effectively than central air or window units, by mechanically creating air flows that the old house was designed to accommodate.

The fan itself is installed in a central hall or near a stairway, and must have attic vents. The part visible in the house is covered with louvers. You see no bulky equipment inside and no big condensers outside.

The windows on the cool side of the house should be opened enough so that the attic fan can draw in cool air; the windows on the warm side of the house should be closed. The air flow cools the house and exhausts itself through attic vents.

The units are sized by the amount of air they move per minute or cubic feet per minute (CFM). Sea-Breeze of San Antonio manufactures fans in 30″, 36″, and 42″ sizes—the largest fan moves 13,200 cubic feet of air per minute and will cool an old house as large as 2,500 square feet. If the old house is two-story, the upstairs windows are closed during the day while the air is drawn into and through the downstairs area. At night, the downstairs windows are closed and the upstairs windows are opened.

You need 1.5 square feet of attic vent for each 1,000 CFM of your unit: for a 6,000 CFM unit, you would need 9 square feet. This can be accomplished several ways: In one large opening with a cover of some sort to keep rain out (and covered by screen and bars to keep all kinds of vermin out), or through gables, or under the eaves. Roof style would determine the kind of vent you need.

The constantly moving air flow created by the attic fan feels cooler and dryer than still air and makes living in an old house a pleasant experience for the operational expense of a 200-watt light bulb.

ATTIC VENTILATING FANS

The other type of attic fan—the one that actually exhausts hot air out of your attic—is mounted on the roof. This one is essential to have if you use ceiling fans in your home. While the ceiling fans cool individual rooms, the attic exhaust fan cools the attic which means that you do not have a layer of air as hot as volcanic ash sitting over your head that acts as a poultice on your living space.

With air conditioning, this type of attic fan is as important as the air conditioning unit itself. Without it, your cool air will use up its energy trying to cool down the ceiling, and your utility bill will reflect this struggle.

Epilogue

IF OUR RESTORATION was a success, it was because Jim and I both love old houses. The right old house can cause your heart to skip a beat. (So can stroke and angina pectoris but the restoration of an old house is more fun.) At first we were not smitten with the house we restored because it was too big. But it had the age, and it had the rocks, and, in time, it had our name on the contract. Today we can't imagine living any place else.

Also, Jim and I work well together. We didn't realize what the secret was until a few years ago when we were redoing the retirement cottage in San Antonio. One afternoon it was very quiet, as it usually is when we work, and I said to Jim, "Gee, I really like working with the paint roller. The paint goes on so fast." Jim was sitting on the floor painting the baseboard and said, "Well, I'd a whole lot rather do the little stuff."

I want a job that shows splashy progress after I've been with it a few hours, and he prefers to do the monotonous, painstaking, finish jobs.

If, when we started a job, he'd yell, "It's my turn with the paint roller—you had it last time," and I had to counter with "No, I didn't either have it last time—it's my turn—you always get the fun jobs," we might have wasted a lot of time going for the jugular.

If we had this restoration to do again, we'd buy a small trailer that would be big enough and comfortable enough (no sand in the borscht) for the two of us and the girls. After all the plaster stages and floor sandings were out of the way, then we could have moved into the house and sold the trailer. It seems to us now, in retrospect, that it might have been simpler that way. On the other hand, if we had not lived through purgatory perhaps we would not appreciate the finished house as much as we do.

Earlier I said that just one one-hundred-year-old house is enough to restore. That is true after you sign the papers, and again when you have only enough life savings left to buy a hamburger and take in a show. That is true during the plastering pits and when you're bathing in the kitchen sink. It is not true when you have nailed the last piece of trim in place and realize you are far more skilled at that point than you were when you started, and what a waste of all this hard-earned knowledge it would be if not put to use again.

Much of the reward of restoration is in the doing, in the actual day by day successes and failures and discoveries. Progressing from the "before" through the "impossible" to the "after" keeps you up nights thinking about what kind of trim the bathroom needs, or how to go about finishing the upstairs floors, but you are never bored. I don't get a flashback of the kitchen as it was every time I get a cup of coffee, but occasionally I pull out the progress pictures and can't believe we came this far.

Restoration is much like the phoenix getting his act together. When that bird's spirit was mucking around in the ashes, his outlook on life probably wasn't too keen, but when he took to the air, he was magnificent. When your restoration is going through the plaster pits, it's hard for your spirits to soar. But when the place is finished, you can only stand back and say, "How magnificent."

Jim's curved spine has not improved with age, but our restoring another house really doesn't depend upon that. Our restoring another house depends upon how soon Jim catches a glimpse of the phoenix soaring over a derelict cut limestone with a tin roof, a passel of boarded-up windows, and a "for sale" sign tacked to the porch.

Appendix

DOWN COMFORTERS
L. L. Bean, Inc.
Freeport, Maine 04033

The Horchow Collection
Box 34257
Dallas, Texas 75234

Eddie Bauer
Fifty and Union
Box 3700
Seattle, Washington 98124

A Touch Of Class
North Conway, New Hampshire 03860

PLUMBING FIXTURES
Renovator's Supply, Inc.
Millers Falls, Massachusetts 01349

Sunrise Specialty
2210 San Pablo Avenue
Berkeley, California 94702

STAIN, FURNITURE KITS
Cohasset Colonials
Cohasset, Massachusetts 02025

TOOLS, STAINS, FILLERS
Woodcraft
41 Atlantic Ave.
Woburn, Massachusetts 01888

Brookstone
127 Vose Farm Road
Peterborough, New Hampshire 03458

Garrett and Wade
161 Avenue of the Americas
New York, New York 10013

MAGAZINES AND JOURNALS
Victorian Homes
Box 61
Millers Falls, Massachusetts 01349

Texas Homes
3988 North Central Expy.
Suite 1200
Dallas, Texas 75204

Old House Journal
69A Seventh Avenue
Brooklyn, New York 11217

STOVES
Woodstock Soapstone Co., Inc.
Route 4, Box 223/296
Woodstock, Vermont 05091

Vermont Castings
Randolph, Vermont 05060

Jøtul U.S.A.
P. O. Box 1157
Portland, ME 04104

Cedar Swamp Steamer
Cedar Swamp Stoneware Co.
1645 Main Street
West Barnstable, Massachusetts 02668

ATTIC FANS
Sea-Breeze Manufacturing Co.
8312 Broadway
San Antonio, Texas 78209

TAX INFORMATION
United States Department of the Interior
National Park Service
Washington, D.C. 20240

Designed by Whitehead & Whitehead, *Austin*
Calligraphy & Illustrations by Barbara Whitehead
Set in Goudy Oldstyle *by* Typesetters Unlimited, *San Antonio*
Printed & bound by Thomson-Shore, *Dexter, Michigan*